DEATH SET

On a golfing holiday, playwright and criminologist Trevor Lowe and his assistant are on their way to see Sir Reginald Allerdyce. They encounter an old friend, Detective-Inspector Shadgold, investigating a criminal known as the diamond bandit and three robberies committed in four weeks — all involving diamonds. When Lowe discovers that Sir Reginald has been murdered, he suddenly becomes involved in the case. So begins a chain of events that plunges all three of them into deadly danger . . .

GERALD VERNER

DEATH SET IN DIAMONDS

Complete and Unabridged

LINFORD
Leicester

First published in Great Britain

First Linford Edition
published 2012

British Library CIP Data

Verner, Gerald.
  Death set in diamonds. - -
(Linford mystery library)
1. Detective and mystery stories.
2. Large type books.
I. Title II. Series
823.9'12–dc23

ISBN 978–1–4448–1295–4

Published by
F. A. Thorpe (Publishing)
Anstey, Leicestershire

Set by Words & Graphics Ltd.
Anstey, Leicestershire
Printed and bound in Great Britain by
T. J. International Ltd., Padstow, Cornwall

This book is printed on acid-free paper

1

'You take the suitcase and I'll bring the briefcase and the golf clubs,' said Trevor Lowe. He swung the bag of clubs over his shoulder, adjusted his tweed cap more comfortably, and picked up the briefcase. His secretary, Arnold White, gripped the heavy suitcase and followed the dramatist along the tiny platform of the village station.

The train that had brought them from the junction snorted and puffed its way along the single track, which was all that Long Norton boasted. Arnold gave up their tickets to the old man who formed the sole staff of the little station, and walked through the microscopic booking-hall. A decrepit taxi was drawn up in the small yard in front of the entrance.

With the assistance of the ancient driver and the equally ancient railway official, the rest of the luggage was piled on the creaking vehicle.

After a strenuous winter and spring, during which he had completed a new play, the dramatist had decided that both he and his secretary needed a holiday. They had chosen Long Norton because there was an almost perfect golf course near the completely unspoiled village, and Lowe was an enthusiastic devotee of the game when he could find time to play.

The journey from London had been hot and tedious. He would have come by car but it was being re-sprayed and serviced. So they had travelled by train. Long before the journey was over, he came to the conclusion that the railways were rapidly deteriorating. The service was not a patch on what it had been under the competition of private enterprise. Nationalisation always led to less efficiency, waste of money, and huge losses. The railways made a profit when they were privately owned and now they cost the country millions.

He gave a sigh of relief as he stepped into the old cab, and settled on the sagging seat.

'It's good to breathe the country air,

Arnold,' he remarked, 'and this is one of the prettiest villages still to be found in poor old England. Look at the mist hanging over those moors and let your soul be soothed and your eyes rested.'

Arnold White nodded.

'The whole place looks charming,' he said. 'I hope nothing crops up to spoil our holiday.'

Lowe looked at him quickly and smiled.

'Thinking of past experiences, eh?' he said. 'I should think that we'd be pretty safe in this out of the way corner.'

Trevor Lowe was an ardent criminologist as well as a successful playwright. His clear brain and insight had helped his friend Detective-Inspector Shadgold on several occasions, and he liked to pit his wits against some difficult and unusual problems. He had solved many, and Shadgold had come to look upon him as a last court of appeal that always produced the right verdict.

However, Shadgold was far away in the dust and fumes of London. Trevor Lowe leaned back against the lumpy cushion and closed his eyes in the drowsy heat of the afternoon. The old cab rattled along at little more than a walking pace, and White was treated to a vista of beauty that only England on a summer afternoon can provide. It was a treat for weary, traffic-tired eyes, a feast of rich browns and delicate greens, heather mauve, and soft greys, stretching out on either side in undulating moorland. Here and there, cattle grazed contentedly, their rich chestnut hides smearing great blots of colour on the softer tones with which nature had painted the landscape, somewhere to the right, a beast lowed, and far away in the dim distance, wafted to them on the stillness of this peaceful world, a church clock began to strike five.

Presently the car swung down a long white ribbon of road, and the country suddenly changed. Houses appeared — snug little cottages, nestling comfortably in flamboyant gardens, the thin spire of a church cleft the skyline, a pointing finger, showing dimly through clustering trees. The road broadened into a street with a little bridge, underneath which a small stream tumbled musically over a rocky bed. More houses came into view, lining the road with walls of rose-coloured brick and grey stone, creeper-clad, and with masses of blossom foaming in the gardens.

Before a timber-faced cottage the ramshackle cab at last drew up, and the driver got down.

'This be Mrs. Jowler's, sir,' he wheezed. 'She's acomin' out now.'

Trevor Lowe and White got out of the taxi just as the cottage door opened and they were greeted by a cheery little woman whose cheeks rivalled the roses that clustered about her. Around her ample form a snowy apron clung lovingly.

'Mr. Lowe?' she said.

The dramatist nodded.

'And this is my secretary, Mr. White,' he answered. 'You've a very lovely little place, Mrs. Jowler. We're in luck.'

'And also very hungry,' added Arnold White. 'I understand that Yorkshire is noted for its high teas.'

Mrs. Jowler beamed at him.

'It's all ready. The tea only wants to be wetted.'

With the doubtful assistance of the aged cabman, their luggage was piled in the small hall. White paid the old man, adding a substantial tip, and the cab jerked and rattled away.

'I'll have the heavy luggage taken up to your rooms as soon as my son comes 'ome,' said Mrs. Jowler. 'If you'll come this way I'll show you your rooms, sir. There's 'ot water in the basin.'

'Splendid,' exclaimed the dramatist. He picked up his briefcase and White took the suitcase. Mrs. Jowler led the way up the narrow staircase.

'This is your room, sir,' she said opening one door, 'an' this is yours, sir.'

'Next door, eh?' remarked Lowe. 'Good! Put down that suitcase in my room.'

White complied. The room was oak-raftered, with leaded paned windows overlooking a rolling expanse of moorland. It was spotlessly clean and smelt faintly of lavender. The furniture was of oak, black with age, and made when men were craftsmen and took more interest in their trade than in their pay packet. A touch of modernity was the washbasin with running hot and cold water which had been obviously recently fitted and of which Mrs. Jowler was obviously extremely proud.

Trevor Lowe hummed a little tune while he washed, in sheer lightness of spirit. He had been looking forward to this holiday for a long time. In another month his new play would go into production and then there would be endless arguments and frayed nerves, late nights, and snatched meals at all hours, but for the moment he was determined to soak himself in the peace of the country.

No premonition came to him of the sinister things that were shortly to take place in this lovely spot. Yet, at that exact moment, across the hills and down in the valley where the twisted chimneys of an old house thrust up among the trees, a web was being woven that was to draw him into as difficult a business as he had ever been mixed up in.

He had a week of real rest, however,

before the spider at the centre of the web moved, and death stretched out a cold hand to pluck a victim from amid the drowsy peace of the village — a week during which Trevor Lowe's pale cheeks tanned and the hollows under his eyes filled out and disappeared.

Days of untroubled leisure, golf, good weather, good food, and a comfortable bed, made him feel a new man. He spent most of his time out of doors. He had become a temporary member of the local golf club, and it was here that he met Sir Reginald Allerdyce, a big, bluff, jolly man, with a ringing laugh that could be heard all over the club, and twinkling blue eyes that shone with a glint of humour. He invited Trevor Lowe to dine at Abbey Lodge, his big house in the valley. His daughter, Pamela, a pretty girl just out of her teens, with eyes that reminded Arnold White of wood-violets — a description that his employer, when he heard it, put down to his secretary's susceptible nature which was always apt to make him extravagant with similes.

Pamela was engaged to Captain Glenister, a dark, rather saturnine man, several years older than she, who was staying at the Lodge. Most evenings, when the purple dusk gathered over the moors, they would congregate on the stone terrace of the house and smoke and chat until it was time to stroll back to Mrs. Jowler's cottage.

Sir Reginald's brother, Doctor Allerdyce, would sometimes join them and relate the latest gossip from the village. He was very like his brother in appearance, and Lowe discovered that there was only two hours difference in the time of their birth — a difference that had given the elder man the title.

Lowe and White thoroughly enjoyed that preliminary week of their holiday. No shadow of what was to come marred their peace, and they had no inkling that the scarlet thread of murder was beginning to wind its way through that pleasant countryside.

The first episode in the forthcoming series of events occurred on the eighth day of their stay. They had risen early, and after breakfast, had set out for the golf course where they had arranged to meet Sir Reginald Allerdyce. As they came to the bridge over the little stream they saw a man coming along the road toward the cottage.

It was White who first caught sight of the broad, thick-set figure.

'Surely it can't be Inspector Shadgold?' he exclaimed in surprise.

'Eh?' Lowe who had been lost in thought raised his eyes. 'Good heavens! It *is* Shadgold! What the devil is he doing here?'

'Bang goes our holiday!' thought Arnold White. Aloud he said: 'How did he find out we were here?'

'He can't have,' declared the dramatist. 'Nobody knows where we are . . . '

They were rapidly drawing nearer to the burly figure who was trudging wearily along. The next second he had seen them and stopped dead in his tracks.

'Well, I'll be damned!' he gasped.

'Probably!' retorted Trevor Lowe. 'What are you doing here, Shadgold?'

'I could ask you the same question,'

10

replied Shadgold. 'I'm here on business . . . '

'And we're on holiday,' broke in Lowe.

'At least we *were*,' said White.

Shadgold took off his hat and wiped his damp forehead.

'You look hot,' said Lowe.

Shadgold snorted.

'Hot?' he grunted. 'I feel as if I'd been boiled slowly! This is a benighted place! Don't they have any cabs?'

'There's one decrepit taxi, vintage about nineteen twenty,' replied Lowe. 'You'd better come back with me to the place where we're staying. It's only a short distance. I've got some beer.'

'Lead me to it, Mr. Lowe!' broke in Shadgold fervently.

It was arranged that White should go on to the golf club and apologise to Sir Reginald, and a few minutes later, Lowe and the detective-inspector were seated in Mrs. Jowler's cool sitting room, and the dramatist had set a large glass of foaming ale in front of his friend.

'Now,' he said, lighting a cigarette, 'tell me what on earth you are doing here?'

Shadgold removed his florid face from the nearly empty glass and wiped his lips.

'It's the diamond bandit,' he answered. 'He's been busy — very busy. The other night Lady Vernon's house was broken into and every diamond she possessed stolen. She'd taken 'em out of the bank that morning for a big reception . . . '

'And no trace left, eh?' asked Lowe.

'Not a thing!' declared Shadgold. 'There were other pieces of jewellery but they weren't touched.'

Lowe poured his friend out another glass of beer. The diamond thief had been operating for a long time. He took nothing but diamonds and only the pick of these. The Vernon stones were world famous.

'There have been three robberies in the last four weeks,' said Shadgold, 'and not a single clue. The A.C. is getting shirty. I suppose he's got a pretty good reason. It's a bad business. The butler at the Howard's was shot dead . . . '

'Always diamonds,' murmured Lowe. 'Nothing else — only diamonds . . . '

'That's right,' grunted Shadgold. He

12

took a gulp of beer. 'And they've all vanished. There's been no sign of 'em among any of the known fences . . . '

'The Vernon's house in Eaton Square is a long way from the village of Long Norton,' remarked Lowe. 'So why are you here?'

'I'll tell you,' said Shadgold. He reached out and took a cigarette from the box on the table. 'I've an idea that this feller has got a hideout here.'

'Why?' asked the dramatist with interest. 'I thought you said there was no clue . . . '

'Nor is there, not to his identity,' interrupted the inspector, blowing out a cloud of smoke. 'But we've discovered that he uses a car, a black Spander. Every station has been on the lookout for it. We don't know the number, of course, but Spander cars are pretty rare. Of course, the usual reports have come in from different places of a car answering to the description having been seen in that particular neighbourhood, but they all, turned out to be fruitless. From this district, however, we've had several reports of a black Spander having been seen on the roads late at night or very early in the morning. Twice the local police have tried to stop it but the driver has refused to obey any signal. I thought I'd come down and have a look round. Never expected to find you here.'

'Well, I wish you luck,' said Lowe. 'It's not in my line but if I can help you only have to ask.'

'That's very good of you, Mr. Lowe,' said Shadgold. 'I may take advantage of that.'

'Have you fixed anywhere to stay?' asked the dramatist, and the other shook his head. 'Then why not put up here? There's another room free and you'll be more comfortable here than at the local inn.'

'That's a very good suggestion,' said Shadgold heartily. 'I'd like nothing better, if you could arrange it.'

'We'll ask Mrs. Jowler now,' said Lowe, and rang the bell.

Mrs. Jowler was only too delighted to take in another lodger. It was agreed that Shadgold should have his meals with

Lowe and White, and he arranged to collect his baggage from the station where he had left it.

'That's settled then,' said Lowe when the beaming Mrs. Jowler had gone back to her kitchen. 'You may as well walk part of the way with me to the golf course. The station's on the way.'

But they only got as far as the garden gate.

A figure was running down the road toward them, the figure of Arnold White. He was breathless and moving jerkily as though he were almost all in.

'Hello, I wonder what's the matter?' said Lowe, as his secretary came nearer. 'Arnold looks very agitated. Something's happened . . . '

White reached the gate, staggered, and put out a hand to steady himself.

'Take it easy,' said his employer. 'What's the matter?'

Arnold White strove to recover his breath. He drew in air in great gulps, but it was some time before he could utter a word. And then he said, with long pauses between each word: 'It's . . . Sir

Reginald . . . Doctor Allerdyce . . . it's . . . terrible . . . '

He stopped, gasping weakly.

'What's happened to Doctor Allerdyce?' asked Lowe.

'It's Sir Reginald . . . He's dead.' This time White was able to speak more clearly. 'He's dead. He was found dead in his study . . . this morning . . . '

'Dead?' exclaimed Trevor Lowe. 'Good heavens! What was it — heart?'

Arnold White shook his head.

'It was murder!' he answered. 'He'd been stabbed!'

Trevor Lowe shot a quick glance at Shadgold but the inspector was staring at Arnold White and failed to see it.

'Murder, eh?' he remarked. 'Have the police been informed?'

White nodded. He had recovered from his exertions.

'Yes, I believe so,' he said. 'Doctor Allerdyce sent for them.'

'I think we ought to go up to the house,' said the dramatist. 'This may be up your street, Shadgold . . . '

'Can't interfere with the locals unless

I'm asked,' grunted the inspector.

'Unless you happen to be working on the case already,' murmured Lowe meaningfully.

'By gosh, d'you think there's any connection?' said Shadgold.

White looked from one to the other curiously.

'Connection with what?' he demanded.

'We'll tell you on the way to Abbey Lodge,' said his employer. 'We'd better get along.'

On the way to the house, Shadgold repeated what he had already told Lowe.

'I should certainly think there was a connection,' remarked the secretary. 'And if you want my opinion, I should say Captain Glenister's the fellow to keep your eye on.'

'What makes you say that?' asked the dramatist.

'I didn't like him much when we met him the other night,' answered White. 'I'd believe anything about him.'

Lowe smiled.

'Except that both in name and appearance he's rather reminiscent of the villain in the old-fashioned melodrama, I can't see there's any evidence against him.'

'Who is this feller Glenister?' asked Shadgold.

'He's engaged to Pamela Allerdyce, the dead man's daughter,' replied Lowe. 'He's a Captain in the Royal Sevenacre Fusiliers, tall, well set-up, black hair and moustache, public school type. Rather a peculiar manner, though. A kind of ultra-superior manner that's a little irritating . . . '

'Looks at you as if you were a nasty smell,' added White. 'Anyway, he had a pretty big row with Sir Reginald last night. Went at it hammer and tongs, I believe.'

'Who told you this?' asked Lowe sharply.

'Leeker, the butler, told me . . . '

'Have you already been to the house?' said Lowe.

White nodded. 'Yes,' he answered. 'When Sir Reginald didn't turn up at the club, I thought I'd go over and leave a message to say that you'd been detained.

Doctor Allerdyce asked me to tell you the news. He said he'd like to see you if you could spare the time.'

'Well, we'll be there very shortly,' said the dramatist. 'I expect they'll be rather surprised to find I've brought a Scotland Yard detective with me.'

Shadgold grunted.

'Don't let on what I'm doing here,' he warned.

'Give me credit for more sense,' said Lowe. 'You're just a friend of mine . . . Here we are,' he added as the gates of Abbey Lodge faced them. 'Come on, and let's find out exactly what happened.'

They walked quickly up the shady drive and soon arrived at the big white stone house, set amid well-trimmed lawns, yew hedges and colourful flowerbeds.

Leeker answered the door and ushered them into the drawing room.

'Doctor Allerdyce is expecting you, sir,' said the butler. 'I'll tell him you are here.'

'This is a terrible thing to have happened, Leeker,' said Lowe.

'Indeed it is, sir,' answered the butler, who still looked white and shaken. 'It was

19

I who found Sir Reginald, sir, and a dreadful shock it gave me. The whole place smothered in blood . . . It'll be a long time before I forget what I saw, sir.'

The old man hurried away to inform Doctor Allerdyce of their arrival. They hadn't long to wait. Allerdyce came in quickly. His big face was drawn and white and he seemed to have aged since Lowe had seen him last. But the resemblance to his brother was still marked. Even his voice was like the dead man's as he greeted them.

'I hoped you might come, Mr. Lowe,' he said. 'Our acquaintance has been of the briefest but . . .'

'If I can help in any way, I shall only be too pleased,' broke in Lowe. 'Let me introduce Detective-Inspector Shadgold of the C.I.D, New Scotland Yard. He's an old friend of mine and he was with me when White brought me the news. I ventured to bring him with us . . .'

'I'm very glad you are here, sir,' said the Doctor shaking hands with Shadgold. 'I don't entirely trust the local police to be able to handle this sort of case . . .'

'I'm afraid, I shan't be able to take any active part in the investigation, sir,' began Shadgold, and Allerdyce interrupted him.

'I know, I know,' he said. 'I've read quite a number of detective stories. So I am cognizant of the procedure. However, your help as an adviser will be invaluable. Mr. Lowe's reputation for crime investigation is quite well-known, even in these remote regions. I am expecting Superintendent Drincott at any moment. He was out when I phoned. Perhaps, you would care to see the — er — study?'

'We ought to wait for the Superintendent, sir,' began Shadgold.

'If we don't disturb anything there's no harm in just having a look,' broke in Trevor Lowe.

'I'll take you up to the study,' said Allerdyce. He went over and opened the door. Looking rather dubious, Shadgold followed Lowe and Arnold White out of the drawing room. Doctor Allerdyce led the way upstairs.

Before a door on the right of the first landing, he paused and took a key from his pocket.

'I took the precaution of locking the door,' he said as he stooped and inserted the key in the lock, 'so that nothing should be disturbed until the police had seen it.'

'Quite right, sir,' agreed Shadgold. 'I don't know that we really ought to . . . '

But Doctor Allerdyce had already opened the door and was standing to one side for them to see into the room beyond. Trevor Lowe was the first to cross the threshold, but he stopped just inside and let his eyes rove round the comfortably furnished apartment. In this room he had discussed with the dead man a great many subjects, particularly his liking for old pottery and glass.

'If you can do without me,' muttered Allerdyce.

His voice shook slightly. 'I'd rather not come in. I — I still feel a bit shaky from the shock. I'll go along and see how Pam is. Poor child, it knocked her sideways when she heard the news about her father.'

He turned away and walked along the passage to another room at the far end.

As soon as he had gone the other two joined Lowe and he gently closed the door. Carefully, the dramatist stepped over to the body, which sprawled face downwards over the broad writing table. From under it blood had seeped in a wide pool over the leathern top. Lowe looked down and his face changed.

They heard him draw in his breath sharply.

'What's the matter?' demanded Shadgold. 'You've seen something?'

Trevor Lowe frowned. He didn't answer at once but his long fingers rubbed gently at his firm chin.

'What is it?' repeated Shadgold.

'There's something extraordinary here,' murmured the dramatist. 'He's wearing evening dress but he's without a collar or tie.'

'It was a hot night,' grunted the Inspector. 'He probably took 'em for comfort. Lots of men do . . . '

Lowe bent down closer. Very gently, ignoring Shadgold's muttered protest, he lifted the head of the dead man.

'Help me raise him,' he said.

'Now, look here, Mr. Lowe,' expostulated Shadgold. 'You mustn't move him . . . '

'It won't do any harm at all,' snapped Lowe impatiently. 'We can put him back exactly as we found him. Come, help me.'

Shadgold hesitated. Then he shrugged his shoulders and came over. Between them they carefully lifted the body until it was upright. The stiff dress shirt bulged in the front and they could see the wound — a blood-clotted slit almost in the middle of the bare chest.

'You see,' said Lowe. 'There are no studs at all.'

'Well, I expect he took 'em out,' said the Inspector. 'I can't see . . . '

'Obviously you can't,' said the dramatist. 'Or you would see that there have never been any studs in this shirt at all.'

'But he must've been wearing studs,' said Shadgold. 'He wouldn't dress without studs . . . '

'Certainly he wouldn't,' agreed Lowe.

'Then what are you getting at?'

'I'm getting at this. This shirt is a fresh one. It's come straight from the laundry.

The stud-holes are still stuck with starch. Sir Reginald was old-fashioned enough to prefer the starched stiff-fronted shirt to the more modern soft type.'

'It's queer,' grunted Shadgold.

'There seems to be only one explanation,' said Lowe. 'This is not the shirt that he wore during the evening.'

Shadgold peered at the shirt and pursed his lips.

'I suppose, you're right,' he said. 'But I can't imagine where it gets us . . . '

'Nor can I — at the moment.'

Very gently he lowered the body back to its original position.

'Perhaps, he changed later,' suggested White.

'Why should he?'

The secretary shook his head.

'Well, I suppose he must've had a reason,' he said lamely.

'There's something else,' said Lowe. 'All this blood . . . '

'The wound must've bled pretty freely,' said Shadgold.

'Rather significant, don't you think?' remarked Lowe.

Shadgold wrinkled his forehead and scratched his chin.

'I don't know what you mean,' he said. 'Why should it be significant?'

But Trevor Lowe was busy looking about the top of writing table and didn't answer. He moved the few papers that were scattered there, replacing them as he found them.

'There's no sign of a knife,' he muttered, 'so I suppose the murderer took it away with him.'

He moved away from the table and stood thoughtfully looking about the room. Beyond the large writing table in the centre there wasn't a lot of furniture. A couple of easy chairs, a well-filled bookcase, and a cushioned settee constituted the bulk. The window was open and Lowe went over and looked out. It overlooked the lawn and immediately beneath there was a patch of shrubbery.

The dramatist bent to examine the broad sill. But there was no mark of any kind on the white stone. It didn't look as if anyone could have entered that way.

Below the window, inside the room,

was a strip of well-polished floor. This also showed no mark. The window could, apparently, be eliminated as a means of ingress or egress. He turned back to the writing table. The drawers were all locked with the exception of one, and this only contained fresh stationery and a few receipts.

It was Arnold White who made the first discovery, and it turned what might have been a commonplace murder into a problem that took all Trevor Lowe's skill to find a solution.

Shadgold and the secretary had been peering about the room while Lowe had been busy at the writing table. Something that sparkled attracted White's eye. It was under the settee and he stooped and picked it up.

'Look at this!' he cried, holding it out in the palm of his hand.

Trevor Lowe took it.

It was a ring — a woman's ring. A large solitaire diamond set in a platinum setting shaped like an animal's claw. It flashed fire, sparkling in the light from the window, with all colours of the rainbow.

He replaced it in White's hand.

Shadgold came over and looked at it. Then he gave a gasp and his eyes nearly popped out of his head.

'By gosh!' he exclaimed. 'How in the world did that get here?'

Lowe looked at him quickly.

'Why?' he demanded sharply. 'Have you seen it before?'

'No, but I've seen a photograph of it,' answered the Inspector. 'That ring was part of the Vernon collection that was stolen three days ago!'

2

Trevor Lowe stared at his friend.

For once, Shadgold had succeeded in thoroughly surprising him. For a moment there was complete silence while they all stared at the sparkling stone in White's palm.

'Are you sure?' said Lowe at last.

'Quite,' declared Shadgold. 'That's part of the Vernon collection. There's no doubt. That setting is unique. That's part of the stolen stuff right enough.'

Lowe picked up the stone again. His lips were pursed thoughtfully.

'It forces us to a startling conclusion, Shadgold, if what you say is true,' he said.

'That murder and the diamond bandits are connected?' said Shadgold.

The dramatist nodded.

'Yes. You seem to have come to the right locality, Shadgold. This ring must've been dropped by the murderer.'

Lowe stroked his chin thoughtfully.

29

'This is a very peculiar crime. Why did Sir Reginald change that shirt? If he'd changed it for a soft shirt it would have been understandable, but — a fresh stiff-shirt . . . It's remarkable.'

'It doesn't seem to make much sense,' agreed the Inspector, 'but there's probably some simple explanation.'

'No doubt,' said Trevor Lowe. He handed the ring to Shadgold. 'You'd better take charge of this,' he said.

The Inspector took it and stowed it away in his breast pocket. They continued their interrupted search of the room but they found nothing else to help them.

'I wonder if we could have a word with Leeker,' murmured Lowe. 'Ring the bell, will you, White?'

The secretary went over and pressed the button. After a little delay there came a subdued tap on the door and the old butler came reluctantly into the study.

He kept his eyes away from the figure sprawled over the writing-table and remained as near the door as possible, twisting his thin hands nervously.

'It was you, wasn't it, who discovered

that Sir Reginald was dead?' asked Lowe.

The old man nodded.

'Yes, sir,' he almost whispered.

'Tell us all about it,' continued the dramatist. 'I'm rather interested to hear your account in your own words.'

Leeker passed the tip of his tongue over his dry lips. He raised a shaky hand to his forehead and rubbed his brows. For some seconds he was silent, collecting his wits, and then he said:

'I'm usually up just before six, sir, and one of the first things I do is to unlock the front and back doors, pull back the curtains, and open the windows of the drawing room, the dining room, and the study. I do the bedrooms later, of course. I did the same thing this morning, sir. When I came to this room I found Sir Reginald like he is now, sir.' He paused and his voice went husky as though the moisture in his throat had dried up. But he recovered from his momentary emotion and went on: 'I thought at first that he'd been taken ill, and then I saw the blood . . . '

He shuddered and stopped abruptly.

'What did you do then?' asked Lowe.

Leeker swallowed.

'I was too dazed to do anything for a bit, sir,' he confessed. 'It was such a shock. Then I called to one of the maids, Alice, sir, and told her to go and wake Miss Pamela. She was just going up when Captain Glenister came down the stairs. I told him what had happened, and he telephoned to Doctor Allerdyce . . . '

'Is Captain Glenister usually an early riser?'

The butler inclined his head.

'Oh, yes, sir, he's up at all hours.'

'Was he surprised when he heard what had happened?'

'He was thunderstruck, sir.'

Shadgold cleared his throat.

'Was there anything open this morning?' he asked.

'Open, sir?'

'Were all the windows and doors shut and fastened?'

'Yes, sir.'

'There was no sign that they'd been forced or tampered with in any way?'

The butler shook his head.

'No, sir. They hadn't been touched.'

'It was a hot night,' said Lowe. 'Are you sure that none of the windows had been left open?'

'Not downstairs, sir. The bedroom windows would probably be open . . . '

'Was this window open?'

'No, sir, it was shut and latched.'

'And there's nothing to indicate that the catch had been forced,' said Lowe to Shadgold. 'It would seem that no one got in from outside unless it was by one of the bedroom windows.'

'I'm sure no one got in from outside, sir,' declared the butler emphatically.

The dramatist noted the peculiar tone in his voice as he made the statement, but he said nothing.

'When did you last see Sir Reginald alive?' he asked.

'At nine-thirty last night, sir.'

'Where?'

'In here, sir. Sir Reginald was in the habit of taking a glass of brandy at nine-thirty every evening, sir. He asked me to bring it to him in the study last night, sir. I usually take it on to the terrace in the summer, but he said he would be working here, sir.'

'That was the last time you saw him alive?'

Leeker hesitated.

'That was the last time I *saw* him, sir,' he answered.

He slightly stressed the word 'saw' and Lowe took him up on it instantly.

'What exactly do you mean?'

'Well, sir, I didn't see him again, but I heard him . . . '

'You *heard* him? Do you mean he cried out?'

'No, sir, I heard him talking.'

'In here?'

'No, sir, in his bedroom.'

A light of interest sprang into Trevor Lowe's eyes. He looked quickly at Shadgold and back to Leeker.

'What time was this?' he asked.

'It would be about an hour later, sir. Round about ten-thirty, I think, sir.'

'You say he was talking,' said Lowe. 'Do you know to whom he was talking?'

This time it was several seconds before the butler answered. And then, very reluctantly, he said:

'To — to Captain Glenister, sir.'

'You're sure it was Captain Glenister?' put in Shadgold sharply.

'Yes, sir, quite sure,' answered Leeker. He looked a little scared and unhappy. His fingers twitched nervously.

'Did you hear what they were talking about?' asked Lowe.

Again there was a long interval before the old man replied.

'They seemed to be quarrelling,' he muttered.

'Did you hear what they were quarrelling about?'

The butler shifted his feet uncomfortably. He ran a trembling finger over his mouth. He said, after another lengthy pause; 'I — I only caught a word here an' there, sir.'

'Tell us,' snapped Shadgold.

'I heard Captain Glenister say 'for Pam's sake . . . ' Then he said something. abut 'the police and restitution' — I think that was the word. Sir Reginald cried: 'It's no use. I'll do what I've said first thing in the morning.' That's all I heard, sir.'

'What happened after that?'

'Captain Glenister said something in a low voice and came out of the bedroom. He looked dreadful. All white and drawn as though he'd had a great shock, sir.'

'Tell me,' said Lowe after a pause. 'How was Sir Reginald dressed when you took him his brandy?'

'In his evening clothes, sir.'

'Was he wearing his collar and tie?'

'His collar an' tie, sir?' repeated the butler. 'I think so, sir.'

'But you're not sure?'

The old man shook his head.

'I think he was, sir, but I wouldn't swear to it. I don't recollect Sir Reginald ever removing his collar an' tie until he changed or got ready for bed, sir.'

Shadgold took the diamond ring from his pocket.

'Have you ever seen this before?' he asked, holding it out.

Leeker looked at it, frowned, and shook his head.

'No, sir,' he said definitely.

The Inspector put it back into his pocket.

'You seem certain,' he said, 'that this, murder was committed by someone inside the house — a member of the household, I mean . . .'

'I never said so,' declared the butler quickly.

'Your attitude implies it,' said Trevor Lowe. 'Do you suspect anyone in particular?'

Leeker shrank back as though he had received a physical blow.

'No, sir . . . No, I don't . . .'

'You don't suspect Captain Glenister?' snapped Lowe curtly.

The butler was silent. With his eyes on the floor he compressed his lips and said nothing.

'Come,' said the dramatist. 'It's obvious from your manner that you do suspect Captain Glenister. Why?'

'I'd rather not say, sir.' The old man raised troubled eyes that were almost pleading. 'I expect I'm wrong an' it might cause a lot of trouble . . .'

'It's your duty to tell us anything you know that might help to clear up this business,' said Shadgold in his best official manner. 'If he's innocent it can't do this chap, Glenister any harm, you know.'

Still the butler hesitated.

'You owe it to your master's memory,' said Lowe gently. 'This was a very nasty crime. It should not go unpunished.'

'It's — it's nothing really, sir,' said Leeker. 'Only that he's been different in his manner lately, Captain Glenister, I mean, sir. He's been very — well, sir, peculiar . . .'

'How do you mean 'peculiar'?' asked Lowe.

'Well, sir, worried and — and moody. Very irritable an' bad tempered — even with Miss Pamela, sir. And then he — he's been out at all hours of the night, sir . . .'

'Is that all?' Lowe sounded disappointed.

'It would be enough — if you knew the Captain as well as I do, sir.' said the butler. 'There's been something on his mind. He — he seemed to be scared of Sir Reginald . . .'

'Scared of Sir Reginald?' repeated Lowe.

'Yes, sir. It might've been that Sir Reginald knew something about him, if you understand what I mean? I can't explain very well, sir . . . '

'I think you've explained very well indeed,' said Lowe. 'So Captain Glenister goes out a lot at night, eh?'

'Yes, sir.'

'In his car?'

'Yes, sir.'

'I see . . . What make of car does he have?'

'A Spander, sir . . . '

'What's that?' demanded Shadgold. 'A Spander did you say?'

Trevor Lowe gave him a warning look.

'What colour is it?' he asked.

'Black, sir.' Leeker seemed rather surprised.

Shadgold opened his mouth to speak but before he had a chance, Lowe jumped in quickly.

'I think that's all, Leeker,' he said. 'I expect you'll have to repeat all this when the local police arrive.'

'Thank you, sir,' said the butler. He seemed to be thankful to be released.

With a slight bow he turned and hurried out of the room.

'Well, what do you think of that?' exclaimed Shadgold excitedly, as soon as the old man had gone. 'A black Spander, eh? The whole thing's as clear as daylight.'

'You mean that Captain Glenister is the diamond bandit, eh?' said Lowe.

'Of course!' declared the Inspector. 'There's not a doubt of it. Everything fits. Glenister is the diamond thief, and in some way or other Sir Reginald found him out, threatened him with the police, and Glenister killed him. It sticks out a mile.'

'I see.' Love smiled. 'As simple as that, eh?'

Shadgold looked at his friend suspiciously. He had heard that tone before.

'I suppose,' he grunted, 'you don't agree? Is that it?'

'Oh, you may be right about Glenister being the diamond bandit,' said the dramatist. 'But with regard to the murder, I believe there's something a great deal more to it.'

'You always look for something difficult, don't you?' said Shadgold.

'I refuse to twist facts to suit a theory,'
replied Lowe. 'You've overlooked two facts
that certainly require an explanation.'

'Two facts?' Shadgold drew his brows
together.

'The fresh shirt and the large quantity
of blood which flowed from the wound,'
explained Lowe.

'Sir Reginald was a very full-blooded
man, sir,' put in Arnold White. 'Isn't it
natural that he would have bled a lot?'

'Oh, yes, quite natural,' agreed his
employer.

'Well, then, what the deuce are you
getting at?' growled Shadgold. 'You've
done this before — all this cryptic
business. Why can't you speak plainly?'

'Because I'd rather not — yet,' said
Lowe. 'If you take the trouble to think
you'll understand what I'm getting at for
yourself.'

There came the sound of footsteps
outside the door and the hum of voices.
The door was opened gently by Doctor
Allerdyce.

He came in, followed by a short, red-haired man with bushy eyebrows and sharp, steely blue eyes. With him was a tall, thin individual, and a stout little man who gripped a bag in one chubby hand and was obviously a doctor.

'This is Detective-Superintendent Drincott,' said Allerdyce, introducing the red-haired man. 'Detective-Sergeant Swires and Doctor Mason.' He indicated the other two men as he spoke. 'Detective-Inspector Shadgold, from Scotland Yard, and Mr. Trevor Lowe, they both happened to be in the district and knew my poor brother . . . '

'I hope, Superintendent, that you will forgive us interfering in your business,' said Lowe, 'but we were naturally interested . . . '

'Please don't apologise, sir,' said Drincott. He held out his hand and gave the dramatist a hard grip. 'I'm very glad to meet you. I've heard quite a lot about your help to the police. I'm very glad to meet you too, sir,' he shook hands with Shadgold. 'I should be pleased to have your advice in this case. Your greater experience will be of very great help.'

Shadgold was pleased — and rather surprised. As a rule the local men didn't like interference unless they'd asked for it, and were not always pleasant about it then.

'I'll be pleased to help — in an unofficial way,' he said.

'That's fine,' said Drincott, beaming happily.

'Now, Swires, just go an' send up the photographer. We'll get a few pictures an' then Doctor Mason can get busy.'

The thin Sergeant nodded and went out.

'If you don't mind I'll leave you,' said Allerdyce. 'This has upset me pretty badly . . . '

'I'm sure that's understandable, sir,' said Drincott. 'Don't you worry. We can get on quite well on our own for the present. I shall want to see you later on, of course . . . '

'I shall be downstairs in the drawing room when you want me,' replied the Doctor. He went out, moving in a queer

43

mechanical way, as though he were sleepwalking.

'Seems to have given him a pretty bad shock,' said Drincott, shaking his head sympathetically. 'Ah well, blood's thicker than water, eh? Must feel it worse because it was his brother.'

The Sergeant came back with the police photographer, and Drincott became briskly businesslike. He explained what he wanted, clearly and succinctly.

Trevor Lowe decided that he was not only a very likable man but also efficient.

The police doctor began his examination as soon as the photographer had finished, and while he was busy, Lowe and Shadgold took Drincott to one side. As briefly as possible they told him all they knew about the matter.

Drincott listened in growing surprise.

'By thunder,' he exclaimed. 'This looks like being a big thing. I was wondering what you were down here for, Inspector.'

'It would be as well if we kept what we know to ourselves for the present,' said Lowe. 'Don't you agree, Shadgold?'

'Certainly I do,' said Shadgold. 'We

haven't enough evidence to make a move, and we don't want to frighten our bird away. That black Spander looks very suspicious for Glenister, but we can't prove it's the car used by the diamond thief . . . '

'That's right,' agreed Drincott. 'We'll have to play him like a fish before we land him. I must say it looks as if he was the feller we want . . . '

The doctor called to him and he turned away.

'The knife penetrated the aorta,' said the police doctor unemotionally. 'Death must have been immediate, or almost immediate. It took place around ten or twelve — any time within that period. Can't be more accurate. I'll write out my report after we've had the body for the autopsy.'

'You can have it within the next half hour,' said Drincott. The doctor nodded curtly and hurried away.

Superintendent Drincott sent for Leeker but he didn't keep the old man long. Briefly he got him to confirm what he had stated to Lowe and Shadgold, and arranged for a room from which he could conduct his investigation.

The butler gave him a small bedroom that was unoccupied. With his sergeant's assistance, Drincott pushed the single bed to one side and arranged a small table at which he could take his notes. Then he sent for the rest of the servants.

Their evidence was negligible. They had neither heard nor seen anything during the night, or at the time the murder was committed.

When he had finished with them, Drincott sent for Captain Glenister. But Glenister wasn't in the house. He had been with Pamela, who was suffering apparently from severe shock brought on by the news of her father's death, but the housekeeper had gone back to her after the superintendent's questioning, and was now looking after her. Glenister had taken advantage of this to go for a breath of fresh air.

'I want to see him as soon as he returns,' said the superintendent to the butler.

'While you're waiting for Glenister,'

said Lowe. 'I'm going for a short stroll. I shan't be long.'

Shadgold shot him a suspicious glance.

'What's he got at the back of his mind?' he muttered to Arnold White.

'No good asking me,' said the secretary shrugging his shoulders. 'You know what he's like. If he'd wanted us, he'd have asked us to go with him.'

'Well, we don't seem to be doing much good here,' grunted Shadgold. 'But I suppose we'd better stay until Mr. Lowe comes back.'

Trevor Lowe walked slowly down the stairs without meeting anyone. In the big hall, however, he came across Leeker. At his request, the butler took him to the side door that led out into the garden.

It was a lovely morning, and the dramatist strolled along a sunlit gravel path, turned a corner, and presently found himself standing under the study window.

There was a mass of flowering shrubs growing in a large bed. Lowe glanced quickly round. There appeared to be no one looking, and he plunged into the midst of the shrubbery.

He began to search about carefully among the bushes, but he found nothing. And then, as he moved the branches of a lilac, something dropped at his feet.

He knew that he had not been mistaken. When he had looked out of the window of the study he had seen a smear of red on the leaves. Something that was wet with the dead man's blood had been thrown out the window. Before he picked it up he saw what it was. It was a long, thin-bladed knife, apparently of Indian workmanship. The razor sharp blade was covered with blood that was still faintly sticky.

He took his handkerchief from his breast pocket and gingerly picked the knife up.

There was very little doubt that this was the murder-weapon. The murderer had drawn it from the wound and thrown it out of the window . . .

And then he saw the initials engraved on the hilt.

N.G. They could only stand for Norman Glenister!

Trevor Lowe stared at the thing, his lips compressed in a thin line.

Here was another and really damning piece of evidence against Glenister. Already there was nearly enough to warrant his arrest. If his fingerprints were found on this knife there was little doubt, that Drincott would arrest him.

Holding his find carefully in the handkerchief, he was backing out of the bushes when a voice behind him startled him.

'Hello, Lowe,' it said curtly. 'What have you found that seems so precious?'

It was Glenister!

He was standing on the path surveying the dramatist with a curve of his thin lip under the moustache. But his eyes were hard in his saturnine face.

His sudden appearance had been unexpected. Lowe was a little taken aback but he kept his surprise from showing in his face. He looked at the cynical face of the captain calmly.

'I think I've found the weapon that was used to kill Sir Reginald,' he answered quietly.

'Have you, by Jove!' Glenister took a step forward. 'What is it?' And then as he saw the knife more clearly. 'Good God, the paper knife!'

'Do you recognise it?' asked the dramatist.

'Of course,' retorted Glenister sharply. 'It used to be mine. My initials are on the hilt.'

There was nothing in his tone but surprise — not the smallest trace of fear. He hadn't so much as changed colour. If he were guilty he was a cool customer, and he had himself under complete control. A dangerous man!

'What do you mean by 'it used to be mine'?' asked Lowe.

'Well, I gave it to Sir Reginald some months ago,' said Glenister calmly. 'He wanted a paper knife to open his letters with. I gave him that.'

'Did he keep it on his writing-table?'

Glenister nodded.

'Yes, it wouldn't have been much use anywhere else, would it?' said Glenister with a slight sneer. 'I suppose the murderer must've picked it up. It's a ghastly business. I'm terribly sorry for Pam. She's taken it badly.'

His face softened for a moment. Then it resumed its habitual expression. Not a very pleasant personality, thought Lowe. He wondered what Pamela Allerdyce could have found in this man to make her fall in love with him.

'Have you found any clue at all to the identity of the killer?' asked Glenister, after a pause.

Trevor Lowe, acting on the spur of the moment, did something then that was very foolish. The moment he'd done it he wondered what Shadgold and Drincott would have to say. More than probably they would both be very annoyed.

'Yes,' he said, 'we discovered a ring under the settee in the study which is undoubtedly part of the collection of diamonds stolen from Lady Vernon's house in Eaton Square.'

This time his words took effect. Glenister's face paled and then darkened as the blood rushed back to his cheeks.

His hands clenched until the knuckles

stood out milk-white.

'How — how the devil could that have got there?' he almost stammered.

'The most likely explanation is that the murderer dropped it,' said Lowe. 'In that case, it looks as though this crime is connected with the diamond bandit who has been so busy during the past few years.'

Glenister had had a shock.

He tried to hide it and made a tremendous effort to speak normally. But his voice trembled slightly.

'It seems rather extraordinary,' he said. 'What could the motive be? Sir Reginald hadn't any diamonds . . . '

'Superintendent Drincott is looking for you, Captain Glenister,' said Lowe. 'Perhaps you'd like to go in and see him now?'

'I'm afraid I can be of little help,' answered Glenister coolly. He had recovered some of his self-possession. 'I'll go in and see the superintendent at once.'

'We'll go together,' said the dramatist. 'I want to show him this knife.'

They walked round the angle of the

house, and into the hall. Neither spoke. They were each fully occupied with their own thoughts. To judge by the expression on Glenister's face his were anything but pleasant.

When they got back to Drincott and Shadgold they were going over the notes, meagre enough, that the superintendent had accumulated. Detective-Sergeant Swires and Arnold White were talking in low tones by the window.

'This is Captain Glenister,' said Lowe as they came in. 'You wanted to see him.'

'Yes indeed,' said Drincott. 'Sit down, Captain Glenister. I should like to ask you one or two questions . . . '

'I know nothing at all that's likely to help you in your investigations,' said Glenister. He sat down easily, and crossed his legs. 'I'm quite ready to answer anything you care to ask — if I know the answer,' he added.

'Just before you begin,' put in Lowe. 'I'd like you to take a look at this.'

He laid the knife carefully down on the table in front of Drincott.

'Good Grief!' cried the startled Shadgold

as he saw it. 'It's the murder weapon!'

'Where did you find that, Mr. Lowe?' asked Superintendent Drincott.

Trevor Lowe explained. He went on to relate what Glenister had told him about the knife, and his assertion that he had given it to Sir Reginald for a paper knife.

'We'll have it tested for prints,' said Drincott.

He called to Sergeant Swires. 'Pack this up carefully and take it over to the station,' he ordered. 'Tell them I want a report on it at once.'

Swires nodded. He took the knife carefully, without removing Lowe's handkerchief, and left the room.

'Now, sir,' said Drincott, looking at Glenister. 'This is rather serious. This knife is undoubtedly your property . . . '

'How can it be my property when I had given it away to Sir Reginald Allerdyce?' asked Glenister.

'It *was* your property, then?' said Drincott.

'I've already admitted that.'

'How do you account for it being used to kill Sir Reginald?'

Glenister shrugged his shoulders.

'It always lay on his writing-table,' he replied in a bored voice. 'Anyone could have picked it up . . . '

'How many people knew it was there, sir?'

'Practically everybody in the house.'

'When did you give this knife to the dead man?'

Glenister thought for a moment.

'About three months ago — it might have been a little more,' answered Glenister.

'You had a quarrel with Sir Reginald last night,' said Drincott suddenly.

Glenister stared at him, but his face had gone a shade paler.

'A quarrel?' he repeated. 'I don't know what you mean . . . '

'I think you do, sir,' said the superintendent quietly. 'Leeker states that he heard high words between you in Sir Reginald's bedroom about ten-thirty.'

'Oh, yes — I remember now,' answered Glenister. 'We did have a small difference of opinion. You could hardly call it a quarrel . . . '

'What was this difference of opinion, sir?'

Glenister looked at him haughtily. The full unpleasantness of his character was in the look.

'That,' he said icily, 'is my business. It has nothing to do with this — this murder . . .'

But Superintendent Drincott, in spite of his good nature, could be very firm indeed.

'I'm afraid that I must be the best judge of that, sir,' he said. He spoke quietly but there was steel in his voice.

Glenister was silent. His mouth under the moustache had set in a thin line.

'Come, sir,' said Drincott. 'Sir Reginald was a friend of yours. I understand that you are engaged to his daughter. Surely you are anxious to help us find the person who killed him?'

'I have nothing more to add to what I have already said,' retorted Glenister. 'If you suspect that I killed Sir Reginald, you're wrong.' He got up abruptly, so abruptly that the chair fell over with a thud. 'I didn't kill him and you can't prove that I did.'

'The superintendent is only trying to find out the truth,' remarked Trevor Lowe. 'Why make it more difficult?'

'I should be obliged if you would keep out of my affairs,' snapped Glenister. 'I can tolerate the police — it is their job — but I draw the line at damned amateurs!'

Lowe flushed. It was offensively said and offensively meant.

Drincott intervened to relieve the sudden tension.

'When you left Sir Reginald's bedroom where did you go?' he asked.

'Straight downstairs into the drawing room,' said Glenister promptly. 'I joined Miss Allerdyce. We went out on the terrace. Leeker saw me leave Sir Reginald's bedroom. I remained with Miss Allerdyce until after eleven-thirty.'

'So you were the last person to see Sir Reginald alive?' said Drincott.

'You are forgetting the person who killed him, aren't you?' said Glenister pointedly.

'Were you and Miss Allerdyce alone on

the terrace?' asked the superintendent.

Glenister's mouth twisted unpleasantly.

'No,' he answered, 'Doctor Allerdyce was with us. He'd been for a walk and joined us soon after my arrival. So you see, it would have been difficult for me to have killed Sir Reginald, wouldn't it? He was alive when Leeker saw me leave him and I was with Pamela and Allerdyce until after he was dead . . . '

'How do you know what time he died?' asked Lowe.

Glenister looked slightly taken aback.

'I don't know — somebody told me it was before eleven,' he answered. 'Why? Was it later?'

Drincott didn't reply. Leaning back in his chair he looked at the man in front of him steadily.

'Do you still refuse to tell us what your quarrel with the dead man was about?' he asked.

'Most emphatically!' declared Glenister. 'I am not bound to answer any questions, you know.'

'That are likely to incriminate you,' ended the superintendent gently. 'If you think the answer is likely to do that, sir, I won't ask you!'

A flush swept up into the Captain's cheeks. Drincott had scored a distinct hit. There are no flies on this man, thought Trevor Lowe, He's got all his wits about him. Shadgold evidently thought the same. A faint smile twitched the corners of his mouth.

'I should like to know,' went on Drincott, 'how long you have . . . '

'Do you think it necessary to keep Captain Glenister any longer?' interrupted Shadgold quietly. 'I doubt if he can help any further.'

Drincott looked surprised but he took the hint.

'In that case, sir, I needn't detain you,' he said. 'I should be glad, however, if you'd remain in the house. We may want to see you again presently.'

Glenister got up.

'You'll find me in the library,' he said curtly.

Coolly and without haste he walked to the door and went out, closing the door behind him.

'Well, he's a perfectly unpleasant feller,' said the superintendent. 'Why did you stop me asking any more questions?'

'I thought you were going to mention the Spander,' said Shadgold.

'I was,' admitted Drincott.

'Better not, at the moment,' said Shadgold. 'Don't you think so, Mr. Lowe?'

The dramatist nodded.

'Yes, I agree that it would be better to keep that up our sleeves,' he said.

'I don't think there's much doubt that Glenister's the man we want,' remarked Shadgold. 'He's the diamond bandit, and Sir Reginald found him out.'

Drincott pursed his lips.

'What about his alibi?' he asked.

Shadgold shrugged his broad shoulders.

'Depends on the doctor being right about the time, doesn't it?' he said. 'It's quite possible that the doctor made an error in the time. Sir Reginald could have been killed later than eleven — after Glenister left Miss Allerdyce and Doctor Allerdyce on the terrace.'

'Maybe,' agreed Drincott. 'That's got to be checked. We've only his word for it at the moment.'

'Miss Allerdyce is too upset to be questioned yet,' said Lowe.

'But there's Doctor Allerdyce,' said the superintendent. 'I think I'll have a word with him.' He got up and stretched himself. 'He said he'd be in the drawing room, didn't he?'

'Yes,' said Shadgold.

Drincott went out.

'I don't think there's any doubt about Glenister,' grunted the inspector. 'Nasty piece of work, if you ask me . . . '

'That doesn't necessarily make him a murderer,' said Lowe.

'You don't think he did it?'

'It doesn't quite fit with all the facts. There are several contradictions. For instance, you say that Glenister is the diamond bandit?'

'That Spander . . . ' began Shadgold.

'We've no evidence that it is the same car that the diamond thief uses. But I'm not talking about that. What I meant is this, surely if Glenister had enough brains to have carried out these robberies and eluded the police for so long, he wouldn't be such a hopeless idiot as to murder Sir Reginald without taking precautions to ensure that he wouldn't be suspected. It's not credible.'

'I don't know about that,' argued Shadgold. 'The robberies are all carefully planned, but this murder was carried out on the spur of the moment . . . '

'You've no evidence of that,' interrupted Lowe,

'How about what Leeker heard? Glenister was hoping to talk Sir Reginald round. When he found he couldn't he killed him.'

'That doesn't explain the changed shirt,' murmured Lowe.

Shadgold snorted.

'To blazes with the shirt,' he cried. 'I don't . . . '

He stopped abruptly. His face changed colour. Lowe swung round toward the door. The sound was muffled but unmistakable.

From somewhere in the house below two shots had been fired in quick succession. Even as they pulled open the door they heard the splintering crash of breaking glass.

They raced out of the bedroom and down the stairs. Frightened voices reached them as they came down to the hall. The butler was trying to soothe one of the maids who was crying hysterically.

'Where did those shots come from?' demanded Shadgold but before anyone could answer him the drawing room door was flung violently open by Doctor Allerdyce.

'For God's sake come here!' he cried as he saw Lowe and Shadgold. 'A terrible thing has happened . . . '

The inspector was at the open doorway first. Lowe heard the sudden hiss of his indrawn breath as joined him and peered over his broad shoulder.

The french windows to the garden were closed, but one of the panes lay in fragments on the carpet. In the midst of the scattered glass sprawled Superintendent Drincott. His face was striped with blood that came from a wound in his forehead. His eyes were wide open and staring and even without the evidence of the bullet hole in the middle of his forehead it was obvious that he was dead!

3

'How did this happen?' asked Trevor Lowe in a low voice turning to Allerdyce. The Doctor was holding on to the frame of the door for support, his face ashen and his whole body trembling.

'I — I don't know exactly,' he answered shakily. 'It all happened so suddenly and — and unexpectedly. Drincott hadn't been here long. He was asking me something about last night — what time I joined Glenister and Pam on the terrace — A shadow darkened the window, there were two shots and a crash of glass . . . Drincott staggered and collapsed on the floor . . . '

'Did you see who it was outside the window?' asked Lowe.

Allerdyce shook his head.

'I only saw a blur. I think he wore a raincoat . . . '

'You didn't see his face, sir?' asked Shadgold.

Again the other shook his head.

'No . . . He had a hat with the brim pulled down. He made off at once . . . '

Shadgold unlatched the windows, flung them open, and carefully stepped out on to the terrace. Over by the balustrade was a small dark object. The inspector took out his handkerchief and picked it up. It was an automatic and the barrel was still hot. He showed it to Lowe who had followed him out.

'Must've thrown it away after the killing,' grunted Shadgold. 'Wonder why he did that?'

The dramatist made no comment. Together they made a search of the terrace in the vicinity, but there were no traces of the murderer. The smooth flagstones were devoid of any marks.

'Granite,' said Lowe. 'Nothing would show.'

Two flights of steps led down to the gravel path that ran beneath the terrace. Shadgold went over to one of these and began to walk slowly down, watching keenly for any signs that the unknown may have left behind. But there was nothing. Nor was he any luckier when he reached the gravel path. Several people had used it and it was churned up with the passage of many feet.

The close-cut lawn extended from the path to a patch of shrubbery; beyond this was a small copse of thickly-growing trees that divided the grounds of Abbey Lodge from the roadway. Lowe and Shadgold examined the ground but there was no sign of anyone having passed that way, although it seemed the nearest way for the unknown to have come.

'Nothing worth our while here,' said Shadgold disappointedly.

They were turning away to return to the house when a man came round the corner of the shrubbery.

It was Glenister. He looked surprised to see them.

'Where have you been?' asked Lowe.

Glenister scowled.

'Really,' he snapped angrily, 'this is getting intolerable! Must I account for all my movements?'

'In the circumstances, sir, yes,' answered Shadgold before the dramatist could reply.

'Detective-Superintendent Drincott has just been shot dead!'

Glenister stared at him. Beneath his tan the skin whitened.

'Shot dead?' he repeated incredulously.

'Didn't you hear the shots?' asked Lowe.

The other shook his head.

'No,' he muttered. 'Shot! Good God!'

'How long have you been out here?' inquired Shadgold.

'Not very long. I came out as soon as I left you.'

'And you heard nothing?'

'No — Oh, yes, I heard the faint sound of breaking glass.'

'You heard that, did you?' put in Lowe. His tone was cold. Glenister was lying! If he had heard the glass break he must have heard the shots. It was impossible that he could have heard one without the other. He didn't press the point but switched to another question.

'Did you see anybody near the house or on the path?'

'Not a soul,' said Glenister. 'How did it happen?'

Shadgold told him.

Glenister listened with a troubled face. He was very clearly upset.

'Dreadful,' he muttered. 'Dreadful!'

There was genuine concern in his voice.

'Yes,' said Shadgold grimly. 'Somebody is going to pay for that.'

'I wish I'd seen the man,' said Glenister, 'but the shrubbery cuts off all sight of the house from where I was. Of course, he may have gone the other way . . . '

'What other way?' broke in Lowe quickly.

Glenister pointed along the path. The dramatist noted that his hand was shaking slightly.

'Where the path turns round the angle of the house,' said Glenister, 'there's a narrower path that joins it further along and leads directly to the drive.'

'Show us,' said Shadgold curtly. They followed Glenister's tall figure along the path and round the corner of the house. The main gravel path ran along by the side of a high privet hedge in which, further along was an opening. The ground here was softer than the path and there, marks of footprints. There were several of them but it was impossible to tell if they had been recently made.

The intersecting path turned through a profusion of bushes, zig-zagging until it finally came out on the broad drive in the front of the house.

'I should think the man must have come this way,' said Glenister. 'There's nothing in the way, you see. If he'd used the copse, which he didn't or I should have seen him, he'd have had to climb two wire fences, both high and made of barbed-wire.'

It seemed to Trevor Lowe that he was doing his utmost to convince them that the killer had come this way. Had he seen the man? He had lied about hearing the shots so he might have been lying about that, too. Another thought struck Lowe. Had it been Glenister who had shot Drincott? He would have had ample time to get rid of the hat and the raincoat . . .

But what motive could he have for shooting Drincott?

Could it be something that the superintendent might have learned from Doctor Allerdyce? No, it could hardly be that.

Other people would question Allerdyce. The death of Drincott wouldn't stop anything coming out that Allerdyce knew . . .

Wait! Could those shots have been intended for *Allerdyce*? This was more likely. But what could it be that Allerdyce knew of which Glenister was so afraid?

It couldn't be his alibi. Pamela was also a witness to the truth or otherwise about that. Was he so sure of Pamela that he was certain she would back up his story? That seemed unlikely . . .

Lowe's brain was working quickly and these ideas passed through his mind with the swiftness of light. He was on the point of suggesting that they should go back to interview Allerdyce when a sudden exclamation from Shadgold made him turn quickly. The inspector gripped his arm.

'Look!' he cried excitedly. 'There's someone over there by the trees!'

Shadgold was right. There was someone — a man lurking among the tall trees, which lined the drive. There was something furtive about his appearance.

Shadgold shouted to him but the man didn't answer. Instead he broke from the cover of the trees and started to run down the drive toward the gates.

The Inspector was bulky but he could move fast. Breaking into a run he went after the man. His quarry wasn't in very good condition for although he tried to put on a spurt, Shadgold was gaining on him by the time they reached the gates leading onto the high road.

And here a disappointment awaited him. As he followed through the gates, the man grabbed a motorcycle that was leaning against the stone wall, jumped into the saddle and kicked the engine into life. The next moment he was roaring away down the road in a cloud of dust.

But for a moment, as he reached the motorcycle, he had looked back and Shadgold had got a clear view of his face.

'Got away, did he?' asked Trevor Lowe,

as the panting inspector rejoined him.
'Pity.'

'Yes, but I know who he was,' said
Shadgold.

'You recognised him?' said Glenister.
'Who was he?'

Shadgold took out his handkerchief
and wiped his perspiring face.

'His name's Barney Berman,'
answered Shadgold. 'But he's better
known as 'Black' Berman because that's
his graft . . . '

'What is?' asked Glenister sharply.

'Blackmail,' replied Shadgold curtly.
'I'd like to know what he was doing here
— I'd like to know that very much
indeed.'

They walked back to the house in
silence.

★   ★   ★

Arnold White was waiting on the terrace.
He had followed them down from the
bedroom at the sound of the shots but
had kept in the background, unwilling to
intrude. If Lowe wanted him he knew

73

that the dramatist would say so. But Lowe had ignored him, and so had everybody else! So he waited, brimming over with curiosity, to know where they had been.

It was Inspector Shadgold who spoke to him first.

'Where's Detective-Sergeant Swires?' he asked.

'I don't know,' answered Arnold. 'I thought he was with you . . . '

'We haven't seen him since he came down with us from upstairs,' said Lowe.

'He didn't come into the drawing room,' said Shadgold, frowning. 'I wonder where the deuce he can have got to.'

As though in answer to the question, Swires appeared at that moment at the open window.

'I've been on the phone to the station,' he said addressing Shadgold, 'and they're sending Inspector Bracken along at once. He'll be bringing the doctor with him. This is a terrible thing to 'ave 'appened . . . '

Shadgold didn't look best pleased. Obviously he thought that Swires might have consulted him before acting so precipitately. He couldn't very well say anything, however, since he actually had no official standing in the matter. Detective-Sergeant Swires had acted within his rights.

'How long are they likely to be?' he grunted.

'They're on the way now, sir,' said Swires.

'H'm. Where's Doctor Allerdyce, d'you know?' said the Inspector.

'In the library, I think, sir,' said Swires. 'His nerves are very bad. He was shakin' like as if he had the ague when I saw him.'

'I'll go and have a word with him,' said Trevor Lowe. 'Poor chap, he's had enough shocks recently to make anyone shake.'

He left Shadgold with Swires to await the arrival of Inspector Bracken, and went to the library. Doctor Allerdyce was there, seated in a chair near the window. He looked years older. A bottle of Hennessy stood on a tray beside him and there was a glass partly full of brandy near it. The Doctor was holding a cigar in his fingers but he had forgotten to light it.

He looked up as Lowe came in.

'Well?' he greeted. 'Anything fresh? I'm afraid I'm not much help to anybody. I feel all in. This last affair of poor Drincott has been too much for me.'

He reached out a hand that was rather unsteady and picked up the glass of brandy.

'I don't usually take this in the morning,' he said. 'After dinner's my time as a rule. But I felt in need of a stimulant.'

He took a drink from the glass.

'You couldn't have anything better,' said the dramatist. 'Perhaps you would rather be alone . . . ?'

Allerdyce stopped him with a gesture.

'No, no.' he said quickly. 'Please stay. Would you care for a spot of brandy?' He indicated the bottle of Hennessy.

'I think I should,' answered Lowe. 'It's been a rather trying morning . . . '

'There's a glass in the cabinet,' said Allerdyce. 'I'll get it.'

'You stay where you are,' broke in the dramatist, as Allerdyce half-rose. 'I can get it.'

He went over to a corner cupboard, a beautifully carved piece of ancient oak, and brought back a glass. Pouring himself out some brandy, he sniffed it appreciatively, took a sip and allowed it to linger on his palate before he swallowed it.

'A good brandy,' he remarked, 'is the king of all drinks.'

He pulled forward a chair and sat down.

'I think you should go home and have a long rest,' he said. 'Get away from these surroundings . . . '

'I'd rather stay,' interrupted Allerdyce. 'Good God!' he burst out suddenly. 'It seems like some horrible nightmare! Yesterday everything was so happy and peaceful, and now . . . It's dreadful, dreadful!'

'You must try and get a grip of your nerves,' said Lowe. He took out his cigarette case and helped himself to a cigarette. 'I still advise you to go home and try and take up your normal life. Carry on with your practice and . . . '

'I don't think I could,' declared Allerdyce, shaking his head. 'I can't leave here until the murderer of my brother has been found and the whole mystery cleared up. I've already telephoned to Doctor Everard asking him to take over my practice. I don't feel equal to attending to patients. My mind wouldn't be on the job.'

'I understand how you feel,' said the dramatist. He lit his cigarette and held out the match to Allerdyce. 'Try lighting that cigar you're holding,' he added. 'It will soothe your nerves . . . '

The Doctor looked at the cigar in surprise.

'Do you know, I'd clean forgotten it,' he said. He took the match, and dipped the end of the cigar in the flame. When it was evenly lit, he blew out a stream of aromatic smoke, and gave a little sigh of pleasure. 'Good tobacco and good brandy,' he said. 'Two of the greatest gifts of the gods!'

'Do you feel equal to answering one or two questions?' asked Love.

'I'm equal to anything if it's going to help,' answered Allerdyce. 'What do you want to know?'

'How long have you known Glenister?' said Lowe.

Allerdyce looked surprised.

'Glenister?' he repeated.

The dramatist nodded.

'About eighteen months, I think,' replied the Doctor. 'It might be longer. I'm not sure. He was Reginald's friend not mine . . . '

'What do you know about him?'

'That's easily answered — nothing at all!'

'Do you know how he and Sir Reginald became acquainted?'

'Well, originally it was the sale of some hounds,' said Allerdyce. 'Reginald, as you probably know, was M.F.H. Glenister was very keen on hunting. That brought them together.'

'I see,' said the dramatist. He paused and then went on: 'What is Glenister's financial position?'

Allerdyce took another sip of brandy.

'I've no idea,' he replied. 'Fairly well-off, I should say. He's given Pam several expensive presents . . . '

'What kind of presents?'

'That diamond necklace and bracelet she wore the other night at dinner when you were here. He gave her those . . . '

Trevor Lowe pursed up his lips in a soundless whistle. He remembered those diamonds — beautiful stones and certainly expensive. Glenister's income must be large if he could afford presents like that.

'He's rather fond of diamonds,' Allerdyce went on. 'He brought back some very fine unset stones from London a couple of weeks ago.'

Lowe leaned forward with such a sudden jerk that he nearly spilled the brandy he was holding. Here was further evidence against Glenister. There *might* be an explanation other than the one that came to his mind, but it was curious. Diamonds, nothing but diamonds. You could call it 'death set in diamonds' if you liked to be fanciful.

'Where does his money come from?' he asked. 'Is he in any business?'

Allerdyce finished his brandy and put down the glass on the tray.

'I don't think so,' he answered. 'I

believe he has a private income.'

'I see. What is your opinion of Glenister? What kind of a man is he?'

Allerdyce looked embarrassed. He frowned and examined the end of his cigar.

'Well, to be perfectly candid,' he said reluctantly after a pause, 'I must confess that I've never liked him. He has a peculiar manner — a certain brusqueness — that isn't exactly — er — endearing. Pam worships him, of course, but for my part . . . ' He broke off and shook his head.

'Do you believe that he knows anything about this business?' asked Lowe bluntly.

'I've been asking myself the same thing,' said Allerdyce. 'I've a feeling that he *does* know more than he's said.'

'What makes you think so?'

'Nov don't misunderstand me,' said Allerdyce hastily. 'I'm not suggesting that he had anything to do with Reginald's death . . . '

'Glenister has an unfortunate manner,' said Lowe. 'With the exception of Miss Allerdyce he seems to be very unpopular with everybody. The servants included.

However, so far as the murder is concerned, he has a good alibi. Sir Reginald was undoubtedly alive when Glenister left him last night. He went straight down to the terrace to join Miss Allerdyce, and they were subsequently joined by you.'

'Yes, that is correct,' agreed Allerdyce. 'I had already said goodnight to Reginald, who was going to work on some of the estate accounts in his study. I went along to the kennels to have a look at one of the hounds, which was ill. Greach, the kennel-man, thought it should be destroyed. I was there for a few minutes and then I came back and joined Pam and Glenister on the terrace. It was just a quarter to eleven then.'

'Why are you so sure about the time?'

'The church clock struck the three-quarters,' said Allerdyce.

Lowe sighed.

Glenister had left Sir Reginald in his bedroom at ten-thirty. Even if the baronet had gone straight to his study there would have scarcely been time for Glenister to have killed him. He might just have done it. Fifteen minutes was quite a long time really. It depended on what time Glenister had joined Pamela. Only the girl could answer that.

'How is Miss Allerdyce?' he asked.

'She's still suffering from shock. She was asleep when I last saw her. Best thing for her.'

Lowe drank some of his brandy. He stubbed out the cigarette he'd been smoking in an ashtray, and frowned. Then he said:

'There's a very curious point that worries me,'

'Only one?'

'One in particular. When I saw the body of Sir Reginald he was wearing a fresh dress shirt . . . '

Allerdyce stared at him.

'A fresh dress shirt?' he repeated.

'Yes. He wasn't wearing either his collar or his tie. Otherwise, he was fully dressed in dinner jacket, etc. Why do you think he put on a fresh shirt?'

'Perhaps he upset something over the other,' suggested Allerdyce. 'He was rather particular about his appearance.'

'He hadn't put in his studs or his links,' said Lowe. 'Surely he would have done that first?'

'He might,' said Allerdyce. 'I can't see why you should think it important.'

The remark was partly a question but Lowe did not answer it. He changed the subject, mentioning the man who had been in the drive and got away on the motor-cycle. He refrained from telling the doctor that Shadgold had recognised the man.

Allerdyce was interested, but he didn't seem to attach any more importance to this than to his brother's changed shirt. For some little while longer the dramatist remained chatting without, however, gathering any fresh information that was of the least value.

Presently he took his leave of Doctor Allerdyce and went along to the drawing room.

Detective-Inspector Bracken had arrived, together with the photographer and a bucolic-looking constable who appeared to be intensely bored with the whole proceedings.

Bracken was quite a different type to

Superintendent Drincott, both in appearance and character. He was a bony man. His fingers were all knobs and his cheekbones stood out over dark hollows. His eyes were sunken and his high forehead was surmounted by thin streaks of lank black hair that he combed carefully in a futile attempt to hide his baldness.

When Lowe entered the room the photographer had just finished taking his last picture, and Bracken was probing the wall facing the french windows.

Obviously he was looking for one of the bullets fired by the unknown murderer. Shadgold introduced the dramatist and Inspector Bracken gave him the briefest of brief nods. He had succeeded in finding what he was looking for, a little flat blob of metal that had lodged in the wall.

He showed it to Shadgold.

'Missed with his first shot,' he grunted. 'The second bullet is in the body. The doctor will be here at any minute.' He turned his deep-set eyes on Trevor Lowe. 'Is there anything you wish to say to me, sir?' he asked rather pointedly.

'Nothing at all, Inspector,' answered the dramatist pleasantly. 'Where's my secretary, Shadgold?'

Shadgold jerked his head toward the window.

'Out on the terrace,' he said.

'I'm going back to Mrs. Jowler's,' said Lowe. 'I expect you'll be coming along presently.'

Shadgold nodded.

Lowe found Arnold White staring gloomily out over the garden.

'Don't like that chap, Bracken,' he remarked when his employer joined him. 'Brusque sort — full of his own importance. Practically told me to clear out . . .'

'Never mind,' said Lowe. 'There's nothing really that we can do. Shadgold will see that Bracken doesn't put his foot in anything.'

They took the path that led round to the drive and started to make their way to the main gates. The sun was casting dancing splashes of light at their feet as it shone through the filigree of branches that met overhead . . . Just as they were nearing the spot where they had seen 'Black' Berman lurking, Lowe caught sight of something that glittered in a splash of sunlight.

They stopped and went over to the shining object.

It was a cigarette case and lay in the longish grass of the verge. Trevor Lowe stooped to pick it up and the action probably saved his life.

At the instant he stooped two sharp reports split the silence. They came from somewhere behind them and they heard the whine of the bullets as they passed near them.

4

Two more shots followed in quick succession and Lowe dropped flat on his face, pulling White down with him. The bullets droned over their heads, too close to be pleasant.

A fifth shot sent a little fountain of earth spraying round the dramatist's face. The unknown marksman was getting dangerously close.

Lowe wriggled his way into the shelter of a tree trunk, and White followed his example. From this screen he peered cautiously in the direction from whence the shots had come.

But he could see nothing.

On the other side of the drive almost in a line with where they lay was a patch of thickly growing bushes. A faint wisp of bluish haze drifted in the still air, and Lowe concluded that it was behind these bushes that the shooter had concealed himself.

The sound of the shots suggested that a repeating rifle had been the weapon used. As he watched a bird flew to the bushes and was about to settle when it veered away into a nearby tree.

Someone, then, was still lurking there.

There were no more shots, however, and after waiting for nearly five minutes, Lowe took off his hat, put it on the end of a broken branch that lay nearby, and slowly pushed it into view round the angle of the tree trunk.

Nothing happened.

Lowe waited, but there was still no shot or movement, and he got cautiously to his feet.

'That,' said Arnold White, following suit, 'was pretty hot while it lasted.'

'It was, wasn't it?' muttered his employer. 'We don't seem to be very popular with somebody.'

He picked up the cigarette case and slipped it into his pocket. He walked over to the bushes and made a search.

There was ample evidence of some-body's presence there. The soft earth had been trampled down and lying nearby were five spent cartridges.

'Thirty-two repeating rifle,' he said, slipping them into his pocket. 'Our murderous friend has quite an armoury.'

'Why?' asked White.

'He used an automatic to kill Drincott which he very considerately left behind . . . '

'Do you think it was the same man?'

'Almost certainly, I think.'

There was a trail of blurred footprints from the clump of bushes that led away in the direction of the back of Abbey Lodge. They were clearly visible in the soft earth.

'Let's see where they go to,' said Lowe.

They set off over the rough, moist ground. The trail took a circuitous course, twisting in and out of the trees, and it was easy to see that the person who had made it had taken the greatest possible care to keep under cover and avoid the risk of being seen.

Across the corner of the kitchen garden, the trail led them, and then became lost in a paved courtyard that was enclosed on three sides by low brick buildings. Evidently these were the kennels that Allerdyce had mentioned.

Trevor Lowe halted in the courtyard and looked about him. There were several ways the shooter could have gone and it seemed useless to try and follow him further.

The dramatist was just deciding to turn back when he saw a man come out of one of the buildings and advance toward them.

He was an undersized specimen of humanity, with a narrow-jawed face and a sliver of whisker on each cheek. He had a low forehead, and bristling hair that grew patchily. In his hands he carried two pails of something.

Lowe went to meet him and accosted him with a smile.

'Excuse me,' he said, 'is your name Greach?'

The man gave him a surly look.

'That's right,' he growled. 'That's me. What d'yer want?'

'I was wondering if you'd seen anyone pass this way, just now?' said Lowe.

The man spat, and shook his head.

'I ain't seen no one,' he grunted.

'How long have you been here?'

Greach jerked his head toward the building from which he had emerged.

'Bin in there fer the last hour,' he answered.

'Then you wouldn't have seen anybody if they came this way?'

'No, I wouldn't,' said Greach sullenly. 'I bin feedin' the 'ounds.'

'Ah, yes, the hounds,' said Lowe conversationally. 'You've quite a number, I understand?'

'We 'ave that,' said Greach, a little less sullenly. 'Twenty couple an' a couple o' extras what Sir Reginald was walkin' fer the Kennel 'Unt.'

'I believe the long Norton hounds are considered a pretty fine pack, aren't they?'

'One o' the best in the country,' answered Greach. 'But they mean a lot o' work for them as 'as the 'andlin' of 'em. I'm the 'ead kennel-man.'

'Are you, eh?' Lowe sounded suitably impressed. 'Who's the vet?'

'Mostly me,' said Greach. 'Sir Reginald used to do a goodish bit hisself. We've a proper dispensary 'ere, an' we've even our own lethal chamber.'

'Lethal chamber?' repeated Lowe. 'Surely that's unusual?'

'Sir Reginald always does — did,' he corrected himself hastily, 'things in a proper way. Nothin' was too good fer the 'ounds.'

'He was very keen on hunting, wasn't he?' asked Lowe.

'Indeed 'e was,' answered Greach. 'Though a lot o' the improvements 'ere was Captain Glenister's ideas. It was 'im what suggested the lethal chamber. 'E 'ad that building over there converted.'

He pointed to a square edifice of red brick. So, thought Lowe, the lethal chamber was Glenister's idea. He was learning something.

'I should like to have a look over that,' he said. 'I've never seen a lethal chamber.'

'There ain't much to see,' said Greach. 'I'll show it to yer tomorrer; if you like. Can't today 'cos I got one of the 'ounds in there . . . '

Trevor Lowe strolled over and looked at the outside of the building. Greach put down his pails and followed him. It was a very old building. The brickwork had crumbled and the mortar needed re-pointing. There was a heavy iron-sheeted door to the place, which looked rather incongruous.

'What do you use — some form of gas?' asked the dramatist.

'No — chloroform,' answered Greach. 'It comes from that there tank, see? Comes through that tube.'

He indicated a small round-shaped tank mounted on the outside wall from which a pipe with a tap ran down and passed through the brickwork near the ground.

'Comes out inter the chamber in a sorter fine spray,' explained Greach. 'Don't take long ter do the trick. Better'n these injections they use now.'

Trevor Lowe wasn't so sure about that. It seemed to him rather a queer thing for a private gentleman to have. It couldn't have been necessary. Surely they didn't have so many hounds that needed destroying? But he kept his thoughts to himself.

'Well, I must be gettin' on with me job,'

said the kennel-man. 'Can't stand gossipin' all day . . . '

But Trevor Lowe scarcely heard what he said. His eyes were fixed on a portion of the ground in front of the iron-shod door. It was of earth and it was moist with water that had been used to wash down the courtyard. In the thin mud, plainly visible, the toe almost touching the bottom of the door was a footprint. It had been made by the same shoe as the prints in the clump of bushes. It was the footprint of the man who had tried to shoot them in the drive!

So the unknown shooter was hiding in the lethal chamber! That seemed the only conclusion to draw from that footprint.

The surly Greach must be in it; his story of the hound was a lie. Not only that, the kennel-man had also been lying when he said he hadn't seen anyone pass that way.

What should he do?

It would be better to pretend that he had seen nothing. There was no real evidence against Greach. He had no power to force the man to open the iron door, and if he had, there might be another exit to the death-chamber. If he went to fetch Bracken or Shadgold, by the time they got back the hidden man would have made his escape.

'Well,' he remarked, 'it's really very interesting. I must get you to show me more one day. I won't detain you any longer now.'

He put his hand in his pocket and took out a ten shilling note and slipped it into the man's willing hand.

'Thank you, sir,' he said, touching his forehead. 'On'y too pleased to show yer round anytime . . . '

Arnold White, who had watched as a silent spectator, turned as Lowe nodded a farewell to Greach, and followed his employer out of the courtyard.

But Lowe didn't go far. In the cover of a hedge in the kitchen garden he halted.

'Listen,' he whispered rapidly, 'I want you to keep a close watch on that lethal chamber. If anyone comes out follow him.'

White looked at him in astonishment. He hadn't noticed the footprint.

'I don't understand quite,' he began.

Lowe explained quickly.

His secretary's face expressed his amazement, which quickly changed to excitement.

'Greach is one of the gang, is he?' he said.

'Greach has certainly got a lot to do with this business,' answered Lowe. 'I wouldn't say he was one of 'the gang'. I don't think there's a 'gang' as you call it, involved. Now, get busy, and take care of yourself. I'm going back to Mrs. Jowler's and you'll find me there when you want me.'

As he walked quickly away he looked back in the direction of the kennels. Greach had picked up his pails and was going toward the door from which he had emerged, whistling shrilly and discordantly.

Instead of going back the same way as they had come, Trevor Lowe passed through a gateway on the other side of the kitchen garden and came upon another courtyard, smaller than the other, which fronted the garage.

The big double-doors of the garage were open and he heard from inside the splashing of water.

This was probably the place where Glenister kept his car. He went over to the open doors and looked in. There were two cars there, the big Daimler, which had belonged to Sir Reginald, and a low-built, speedy-looking machine shining blackly — the Spander.

It was apparently in the process of being cleaned. The nozzle of a hosepipe attached to a tap in the corner was lying beside the rear wheels and there were dusters and tins of polish on the long running board.

Lowe went closer. Like all the Spanders, of which there were comparatively few, it was a beautiful job. There was nothing of the conveyer belt about it. It was a handmade piece of pure craftsmanship.

There seemed to be nobody about. The garage was a large building with ample room for four cars if necessary, and lit by tubular lighting in the centre of the roof. Lowe leaned over the Spander and examined it with interest.

Was *this* the car that had been used to carry out the diamond robberies? It was by no means a certainty. In his eventful life, the dramatist had learned that coincidences were actually more common in real life than in fiction. Was it just a coincidence that Glenister owned a black Spander?

By itself it could be. But taken in conjunction with the other facts it seemed impossible.

He was so absorbed in what he was doing that he heard no sound to warn him that he was being watched. It was a faint creak and the change in the light value that made him turn sharply.

The double-doors were closing! Smoothly they swept together and shut with a gentle thud. Lowe ran over to them and pushed against them with all his strength.

But they were immovable!

Obviously they must work on some kind of motor mechanism, probably hydraulic. Somebody had made him a prisoner.

It seemed rather a stupid thing to do

because sooner or later the chauffeur would be bound to come back.

And then the centre light went out!

The control must have been outside the garage, It left the place in complete darkness because there was no window. Who was responsible for this nonsense? It seemed like a silly joke. He felt himself growing angry. Somebody must be laughing at him! He had been caught so easily . . .

He tried to stop his rising temper and groped in his pockets for the torch he always carried. He found it, pulled it out, and pressed the button.

A beam of white light dissolved the darkness in its path. He slowly played it round the garage until the light covered every inch of the interior. There appeared to be no other exit but the main doors. He went over again to these doors and tested them. They were firm and refused to budge a fraction.

Lowe shrugged his shoulders. He sat down on the running board of the Daimler, took out his cigarette case and lit a cigarette.

What was the object of this latest exploit on the part of — someone? Was it just a stupid joke or was there some deeper purpose behind it? Was the chauffeur in it? Greach definitely was, so why not the chauffeur?

But whose was the directing brain? Glenister?

If so why was it so necessary that he should be got out of the way like this? Was something about to happen which it was necessary he shouldn't see?

Well, it wasn't too uncomfortable. He had plenty of cigarettes, and somebody was bound to come along eventually.

A faint sound made him look up. Somebody was on the roof! He put on his torch and directed the light upwards.

The roof slanted slightly from a central beam, sloping gently down on either side to the stone walls. A series of thin iron girders strengthened the whole structure.

But there was something he hadn't noticed before. A small, square ventilator was set in one side of the roof. It had been covered over with paint and was practically invisible.

But now it was opening slowly!

He saw the patch of blue from the sky as it rose. An arm darkened the aperture and then something dropped and smashed on the concrete floor.

Trevor Lowe sprang to his feet. The window above shut with a bang and he smelt the strong pungent odour of bitter almonds!

He held his breath!

He knew what that smell meant. Someone had dropped a flask of hydrocyanic acid!

It would rapidly turn to gas and the garage would become a deathtrap! The slightest whiff of that poisonous vapour would mean instant death!

So that was the object. Certainly far removed from a joke!

Still holding his breath, Lowe looked about quickly. He would have to find some way getting out, and quickly. Already his lungs felt as though they were being constricted by an iron band.

There must be a way — there must . . .

The Daimler!

If he could only hold his breath long

enough to try his plan. He pulled out his handkerchief and soaked it with water from the hose and bound it over his nose and mouth. Even with that protection he dare not do more than ease his bursting lungs. The volatile acid that was filling the garage was one of the deadliest poisons known to science . . . stumbling over to the Daimler, he clambered up behind the wheel, switched on the ignition and thrust at the self-starter. His head was throbbing and his tortured chest was on fire . . .

And the engine refused to start!

Frantically he pressed the starter again.

And again nothing happened

He felt his head swimming. He couldn't hold his breath any longer . . . Perhaps there was no petrol in the machine . . .

Desperately he tried a third time . . . And the engine throbbed to life!

Almost at the end of his tether, he pressed on the accelerator hard, slipped the gear into first, and let in the clutch. With a jerk the powerful car bounded forward — straight for the closed doors!

It smashed into them and with a

5

In the meanwhile, Arnold White, unaware of his employer's danger, was carrying out his instructions to keep a watch on the lethal chamber.

He took careful stock of his surroundings and chose as a point of vantage a patch of thick laurels which would not only act as screen from any observer but would also protect him from the hot sun.

To get to his hiding place he had to cross about six yards in the open, across a bed of cabbages. If anyone were looking he was bound to be seen, but he couldn't stay where he was. He would have to risk it. It would only take him a fraction of a minute.

He made up his mind to try. With a sharp look round to make sure that there was no one about, he slipped swiftly across to his objective, dropped on all fours and wriggled his way to the centre of the bushes.

It was an ideal place. He was protected on all sides by thick foliage, and stretching out on his chest he parted the branches in front of him so that he had a clear view of the lethal chamber.

The courtyard was deserted. There was no sign of Greach. The sun streamed down from a cloudless sky on the courtyard and the long row of kennels. He could hear a faint stirring in the kennels and the faint whine of a hound, but that was all.

For over twenty minutes he lay there, trying to keep at bay the sleepiness that threatened to overcome him. Presently he could hear the rattle of crockery from the house. The sound reminded him that he was hungry. He had had a fairly early breakfast.

Food was a pleasant thought!

He began to think of all the dishes he would like at that moment. Mrs. Jowler had mentioned that she was getting them steak for lunch! He pictured it, all juicy and succulent, with mushrooms, potatoes and peas . . . Followed by a cherry pie and thick fresh cream..,

In the midst of these delectable dreams he suddenly stiffened. There was movement in the courtyard. Round the corner of one of the buildings the figure of a man appeared.

Arnold couldn't see his face because he wore a wide-brimmed hat pulled down over his eyes, but he was wearing a long raincoat that reached almost to his heels. Only as some form of disguise would anyone, except a lunatic, wear a raincoat on a hot day like this. It must be the same man who had shot Drincott! He answered perfectly to Doctor Allerdyce's description of the man who had appeared at the french window.

The man moved stealthily round the building, keeping in the shadow, and slipped inside the open doorway through which Greach had gone.

Arnold White got carefully to his feet. What ought he to do next? Should he stay where he was in case the man reappeared, or should he try and get nearer to the building into which he had gone? He decided to stay where he was and keep watch.

It was as well that he did for after a short interval the man in the raincoat came out accompanied by Greach and they both hurried off across the courtyard.

White emerged from the laurel bushes and hurried quickly and cautiously to the entrance to the courtyard. He must try and find out what this man looked like. Either there was another exit from the lethal chamber or Trevor Lowe had been wrong when he thought that the man had been hiding there. Nobody had left the lethal chamber by the iron door.

The courtyard was empty when he reached it. Both Greach and the stranger had disappeared. White paused, undecided what to do next. He had no idea where they had gone. They could have slipped between any of the numerous kennels. If he went too far into the courtyard there was a danger that he would be seen . . .

And then like the blast of a bomb the blue sky exploded in a searing orange flame that seemed to burn into the centre of his brain. A blackness, blacker than the darkest night, wrapped him in an ebon blanket, and he knew nothing more . . .

★   ★   ★

He felt as if the entire top of his head was being crushed between the red-hot jaws of a gigantic pair of pliers.

He opened his eyes but the pain was so great that he promptly closed them again. His whole body ached, culminating in concentrated agony in his head.

He lay still, wondering what on earth could have happened. But his brain refused to function. Something had happened to him but he couldn't piece it together. Perhaps he was in hospital? But the bed was very hard . . . And it was very dark . . .

His senses slipped away again and all thought faded away . . .

He came slowly back to consciousness with a groan. This time when he opened his eyes, the pain was not so severe. His jaws felt stiff but he couldn't move them. When he tried to put up his arm to his sore mouth he found that he couldn't.

This puzzled him. For several minutes he tried to figure it out. And then as his senses cleared a little he found the explanation.

He was gagged and bound!

He began to remember ... the courtyard blazing in the sun ... the man in the long raincoat ...

Somebody had crept silently up behind him and hit him over the head. Who was it? Where had they taken him? He was lying on his back and his fingers told him that he was lying on damp earth. There was a peculiar stale smell that made him conclude that he was in some kind of cellar. He tried to move his legs but found it impossible.

The darkness was intense. He could see nothing at all. It was like being enveloped in a black velvet curtain.

He lay for a little while staring up into the black void. Something fell with a soft splash on his face. He felt it trickle down his cheek. He was puzzled and then the explanation seeped into his dazed brain. It must be moisture from the roof.

This seemed to indicate that he was

somewhere underground. A cellar as he had thought. But where? And who had hit him? It couldn't have been the man in the raincoat or Greach.

It was some third person who had crept up behind him.

After a while he began to feel stronger. The pain in his head was subsiding a little. It was sore but his brain no longer felt on fire.

He tried to loosen the cords that bound his wrists and ankles, but they had been too securely tied.

Well, it looked as though he'd had it! Perhaps, he'd be left here until he starved to death! It wasn't a pleasant outlook, but nobody knew where he was — except the people who had brought him here.

Of course, there was always the chance that Trevor Lowe would find him. He knew that he'd been watching the lethal chamber. He also knew that Greach was mixed up in this business. But it would be some time before Lowe became alarmed at his, White's, absence. He would merely think that he was on the trail of the man from the lethal chamber . . .

A faint sound that seemed to come from a considerable distance away roused him. He listened, straining his ears. But he could hear nothing more. He began to think that he must have imagined the noise when he heard it again.

It was the soft shuffle of an approaching footstep!

He rolled over on his side in the direction that the sound seemed to have come from. Presently he saw a very faint glimmer of light in the distance. It was moving up and down like a will-o'-the-wisp and seemed to be a very long way off.

But it grew steadily larger and brighter as he watched, and presently he was able to see that it was an electric torch.

The rays reflected back from the wet walls and roof of a low-ceilinged passage that seemed to stretch away into infinity.

He wasn't in a cellar then, but in some sort of tunnel.

Nearer and nearer came the dancing light, and now he could distinguish shadowy figures behind the light. As they drew almost level with him, White recognised the one holding the torch as the man in the raincoat. Beneath the soft-brimmed hat his face looked curiously white and featureless. The other man was Greach.

Arnold closed his eyes as the torch was directed on him.

'Still senseless,' grunted the man in the raincoat in a muffled, rather husky voice. 'Well so much the better. Give me a hand with him.'

'He had a pretty hefty whack,' said Greach.

'Pity it didn't kill him,' snarled the other. 'Come on, let's get it done with.'

They bent over Arnold and raised him by the shoulders and ankles. He allowed himself to go limp so that his body sagged. He didn't want them to know that he had recovered his senses. Very cautiously as he was lifted, he raised his eyelids a fraction. The man in the raincoat was holding his ankles and Arnold could distinguish him quite clearly in the light of the torch, which Greach had stuck in his jacket. The reason for the peculiar appearance of his face was now obvious.

He had a white scarf tied over it.

White felt himself swung up between them. They set off in the opposite direction to the way they had come. He couldn't imagine what this place could be or where they were taking him.

After they had carried him for about fifty yards, they stopped and began to ascend a flight of steps. A queer smell, like decaying apples, reached his nostrils. Was this place some kind of storage for fruit?

The man in the raincoat suddenly dropped his ankles, and fumbled in his pocket. Arnold heard the rasp of a key and the creak of a door. The apple smell grew stronger. A draught of air that felt cold and clammy wafted across his face. His feet were picked up again and he was carried forward a little way and dropped on the floor.

'He'll be safe enough here,' grunted the man in the raincoat. 'We'll wait until later before we finish the job. Have you got plenty of the stuff?'

Greach grunted an assent.

'I shall have to fill up the tank,' he said.

'Right, but leave it until it's dark. We've had so many snoopers about, it's better to be on the safe side.'

Greach took the torch from the front of his jacket.

'Might as well be goin',' he said. 'This place gives me the creeps!'

'You're squeamish,' grunted the other. 'Come on, then . . . Not that way, you fool, the other entrance!'

The light of the torch was turned away. White made out the narrow doorway through which they had come. Then the light vanished as the door closed with a thud, and there was silence.

Arnold White felt a cold sweat break out on his forehead. He knew the significance of 'filling the tank', which Greach had mentioned.

He was in the lethal chamber!

★   ★   ★

Trevor Lowe wiped the perspiration from his face after the car came to a jolting stop. He got down from the driving seat of the Daimler and looked about him.

Nobody seemed to have heard the noise he had made in smashing his way out of the garage.

He turned his attention to the car. The contact with the doors had not improved its frontal appearance. The radiator was badly dented and the water was pouring from a burst pipe. The front of the wings were buckled and both the headlights smashed and twisted.

It would take a good bit of repairing. However, it couldn't be helped. And it had saved his life! He went back to examine the garage. There was a light ladder reared against one side. This was the way the unknown had reached the roof with his deadly flask.

Lowe was still looking at the ladder when a shout behind him made him swing round.

A short, thickset man, in his shirtsleeves, and wearing breeches and black leather leggings was running toward him across the courtyard.

'Hi!' shouted the newcomer wrathfully. 'What the 'ell have you been doin'?'

'Are you the chauffeur?' asked Lowe.

'Yes, I am!' cried the other truculently. 'Look at them there doors! Look at the car — all busted up! Nice little game you've bin playin', ain't yer? Who the 'ell are yer? 'Ow did yer get in 'ere . . . '

'Look here, my man!' snapped Trevor Lowe. 'Just you answer me one or two questions. What's your name?'

'I'm not answerin' no questions!' declared the outraged chauffeur. 'Wot I want ter know is . . . '

'It's what *I* want to know that matters,' broke in the dramatist curtly. His usual even temper had suffered from his recent ordeal. 'A serious attempt has just been made to kill me and I want to know who was responsible.'

'An attempt ter kill yer?' exclaimed the man. 'You must be bonkers! What d'yer mean?'

Briefly Lowe explained.

The chauffeur listened, his eyes popping from his head.

''Ere,' he said suspiciously. 'You ain't makin' this up, are yer? You ain't tellin' me the tale?'

'Certainly not,' declared the dramatist.

'I've told you the truth.'

'Cor lumme, what a dirty trick!' cried the chauffeur indignantly.

'I agree with you,' said Lowe drily. 'Now will you tell me your name?'

'Timms, sir. Jimmy Timms.'

'I suppose you've been working in this garage most of the morning?'

Simms nodded.

'That's right,' he said.

'What made you leave it?'

'I went to 'ave a bite to eat an' a cuppa.'

'I see. Do you always go at the same time?'

Timms nodded.

'Mostly,' he replied. 'It's me elevenses, yer see. Gives me a bit of a break.'

'How long are you away as a rule?'

'About twenty minutes to 'alf an hour.'

Lowe was watching the man's face closely, but Timms returned his look without flinching.

'You were longer today, weren't you?'

'That were Greach,' said the chauffeur. ''E stopped me on the way back an' asked me ter 'ave a look at his motor bike . . . '

'Greach, eh?'

'There was nothin' much the matter with it, neither,' said Timms. 'Just a short in the plug lead . . .'

'H'm!' Lowe fingered his chin. 'The doors work automatically, don't they?'

'Yes, sir. There a lever what you pull an' that shuts 'em an' they locks theirselves. You 'as to 'ave a key to unlock 'em. Then they opens when you push the lever . . .'

'How many people have a key?'

'Well, there's me,' answered Timms, 'an' Sir Reginald 'ad one an', of course, Captain Glenister.'

'Oh, Captain Glenister has a key, has he?'

'Yes, sir.'

'He uses his car a lot, does he?'

A look of disgust crossed the face of the chauffeur.

'He's out in it at h'all hours,' he replied. 'Many's the time I've left it all poshed up an' polished at night an' come in the mornin' to find it all over mud an' mess. Don't know what 'e does with the thing. Seems ter like drivin' at night.'

The dramatist thought he could have

119

answered Timms's question.

'Must go a pretty good distance,' went on the man, 'from the state of the car. Oh, well, I s'pose it ain't none o' my business.'

Everything seemed to point to Glenister, thought Lowe.

'Don't worry about the damage,' he said, 'I'll explain to Doctor Allerdyce.'

He left Timms looking rather dubiously at the smashed radiator of the Daimler and walked back to the drive. He was quite certain that the chauffeur had had nothing to do with the attempt on his life. He had answered frankly all the questions he had been asked, and there was something about him that breathed honesty.

But Greach was a cat of another colour. There was little doubt that he was in it up to his neck. The motor bike had been an excuse to keep Timms out of the way while somebody did the trick with the flask of acid . . .

Glenister?

It seemed probable but it was dangerous to jump to conclusions.

At the point where the side path entered the main drive, he ran into Shadgold.

'Hello,' exclaimed the surprised inspector. 'I thought you'd gone back to Mrs. Jowler's.'

'I was unavoidably detained,' answered Trevor Lowe. He told Shadgold what had happened at the garage. The inspector listened with increasing astonishment.

'Good Lord!' he exclaimed when Lowe finished. 'What a damnable scheme! Who d'you think it was?'

'Whoever it was he was very thorough,' said Lowe. 'It was touch and go! If the Daimler trick hadn't worked . . . '

He shrugged his shoulders expressively.

'I'll bet it was Glenister,' grunted Shadgold.

'We've no evidence,' Lowe pointed out.

'What about this chap, Greach?' said Shadgold. 'We could pull him in and make him tell us who's behind all this . . . '

'I doubt if you'd get him to say anything,' said Lowe. 'You can't prove anything against him. Where was Glenister when you left?'

'Upstairs with the girl,' replied Shadgold. 'I was coming back to the cottage to find you. Bracken and Swires are getting on with it, and I've no official status, you know. Bracken hinted pretty clearly that he'd rather handle the case on his own.'

'He's that type,' said Lowe. 'Sees a chance of personal kudos and possibly promotion.'

'Well, he can get on with it,' said Shadgold with satisfaction. 'I haven't told him anything. If he wants to be clever he can find it all out for himself.'

They had reached the gate to the main road while they had been talking, and leaving the drive they turned in the direction of Mrs. Jowler's.

'I can do with some food,' remarked Shadgold. 'You say Mr. White's watching this death house, or whatever it is?'

'Yes, I'm hoping that we may have some news from him that'll help considerably.'

'I hope you're right,' said the inspector.

'We're dealing with clever people,' continued the dramatist, 'and until we've got some real evidence against them, we must go carefully. If we make a false move they'll slip through our fingers. So patience is the order of the day, in my opinion. For some reason the man we're after is in a panic . . . '

'What makes you think that?' broke in Shadgold.

'What else can account for these repeated attempts on my life?' said Lowe. 'He's afraid. He thinks I know more than I do. Now when a man gets in that state, he starts making mistakes. That's what we've got to wait for.'

'Maybe you're right,' grunted the inspector. 'I'd like to know how that chap, Berman, comes into it . . . '

Lowe uttered an exclamation.

'I'd forgotten all about it!' he exclaimed.

He put his hand in his pocket and produced the cigarette case that he had picked up in the drive earlier.

'I believe that this must've belonged to Berman,' he said.

He opened the case. Inside were five cigarettes, a ten-shilling note, and a folded scrap of paper. He unfolded it.

On it, scrawled in pencil, were two words:

'*Monk's Tomb*'.

Shadgold frowned down at the little slip of paper in Lowe's hand.

''Monk's Tomb'.' he repeated. 'What the devil does that mean?' Trevor Lowe shook his head.

6

The first thing that Trevor Lowe did when they arrived at Mrs. Jowler's was to take out one of the bottles of John Haig with which he had thoughtfully provided himself, and pour out two stiff drinks for himself and Shadgold.

'Ah!' said the inspector, when he had swallowed a good portion of the whisky. 'I needed that!'

'Same here,' agreed the dramatist. He put down his glass. 'I don't expect lunch will be long. Meanwhile, let us have another look at the bit of paper.'

He took the cigarette case out of his pocket and, out of the cigarette case, the slip of paper. Shadgold reached out and took it from him.

'If you ask me,' he remarked, after looking at it for a moment or two, 'somebody gave Berman a tip for a race and he jotted down the name of the horse.'

Lowe smiled.

'That's a reasonable suggestion,' he answered, 'but it might be something different, and we've got to keep an open mind. It could quite easily refer to some local landmark or place.'

'If it does, most likely Mrs. Jowler will know,' said Shadgold. 'What I'd like to know is why Berman was lurking about Abbey Lodge.'

'Abbey Lodge?' repeated Lowe thoughtfully.

Shadgold shot him a quick glance.

'Something struck you?' he asked.

'Only that 'Abbey' and 'Monk' go together,' answered the dramatist. He reached out for his glass and drank the rest of the whisky. 'It ought to have occurred to me before.'

'Are you suggesting that this Monk's Tomb is somewhere near Abbey Lodge?' inquired the inspector.

'I don't know,' Lowe got up, went over to the bottle of Haig and poured himself another drink. 'Have another?'

Shadgold drained his glass.

'I won't say 'no',' he replied.

The dramatist held out the bottle of Haig.

'Help yourself,' he said. When Shadgold had done so, rather generously, he went on: 'If this is a place, or landmark, Berman may have been going to meet someone there. Then it might be a kind of password to identify himself to someone, or the Keyword to a cipher — even the combination of a safe with a letter-lock . . .'

'Or a hundred and one other things,' broke in the inspector. 'By Jove, I wish Mrs. Jowler would hurry up with some food. I'm starving!'

'I told her two o'clock,' said Lowe. 'I was going up to the golf club when all this started — remember?'

Shadgold looked at his watch.

'It's nearly that now,' he began and stopped for at that moment a beaming Mrs. Jowler arrived to lay the table.

It was, as the inspector remarked some time later, a meal worth waiting for. And considering the amount he had tucked away, he should have been a good judge. Mrs. Jowler brought in coffee and it was then that Trevor Lowe put his question.

'Have you ever heard of a place called the Monk's Tomb?' he asked.

Mrs. Jowler considered, screwing up her face in an effort of thought. After a moment or two she shook her head.

'Can't say that I have, sir,' she answered.

She departed with a laden tray and Lowe helped himself to a cigarette.

'Well, that's that,' he remarked. 'It can't be very well known or I'm sure she would have heard of it.'

He held out his case to Shadgold but the inspector shook his head.

'No, thanks,' he said. 'I'll have a pipe, if you don't mind.'

He produced a battered briar and an equally old leather pouch and proceeded to stuff tobacco into the charred bowl.

'I suppose,' remarked Lowe after a thoughtful pause, 'the most likely place to gain information about the Monk's Tomb would be the local pub . . . '

'Or the local bookie,' put in Shadgold with a grin.

'Ah, I see that you still put your money

on it being the name of a horse.'

Shadgold, replete with a large meal, yawned.

'It's as good a guess as any,' he said. 'What do we do next?'

'So far as I am concerned,' said Lowe, 'nothing!'

'Well, I must admit that's what I feel like,' said the inspector, puffing at his pipe, which seemed in danger of going out. 'But I suppose I shall have to keep in touch with what's going on.'

'I intend to go up to my room and spend the afternoon in thought,' said Lowe.

'Which means you're going to sleep, I suppose?'

'Nothing of the kind. I really mean 'think'. I never believe in just doing something for the sake of doing something. There's no point in it. The first thing is to evolve a plan. When that's done *then* is the time for action.'

He rose and went over to the door.

'I'll see you later,' he said, and went out.

Shadgold looked at the closed door,

transferred himself from his chair to an easy one by the fireplace, hooked a smaller chair nearer, and put his feet up . . .

When Mrs. Jowler looked in an hour later, Detective-Inspector Shadgold was fast asleep and snoring loudly!

★   ★   ★

Trevor Lowe made his way slowly up the stairs, entered his bedroom and closed the door. He pulled an armchair over to the open window, settled himself comfortably, and gave himself up to thought.

The afternoon dragged slowly by but he scarcely moved except to light another cigarette. With his eyes half-closed and his brows drawn together in a wrinkle of concentration, he went carefully over all the facts in his possession. It was something like plotting a new play except that he couldn't invent any facts. He had to use the ones that existed to evolve his plot.

Utterly absorbed in his thoughts, and completely unaware of his surroundings, he mentally reviewed the events of the past few hours.

And there was certainly no lack of material.

Things had happened both fast and furious!

So far as the diamond bandit was concerned, he admitted that it wasn't his line of country at all. That sort of thing was better left to the police who were better able to cope with it.

But the murder of Sir Reginald Allerdyce was different.

Although it was undoubtedly connected with the diamond thief it was the kind of crime that appealed to him. There were points about it that lifted it out of the ordinary. He felt that he held the hub of the whole problem in his hand.

And the hub was that changed shirt . . .

There might be many spokes radiating from that hub but the important thing was the centre of the wheel of intrigue. All the rest would spin easily and smoothly once he got the hub right.

Gradually as he sat there in the heat and stillness of the drowsy summer afternoon, smoking cigarette after cigarette, until the ashtray at his elbow was piled high with stubs, the soft flower-scented breeze blowing gently in at the open window, he began to evolve a theory.

It was such a startling theory that when it first loomed out of the mists of his mind he discarded it as absurd. It was too incredible . . .

And yet — was it?

He went over all he knew and the facts fitted. What had at first seemed so ridiculous became less so as it was put to the test.

He had been so deeply engrossed in his thoughts that he discovered that it was five o'clock with a start of surprise. He had a wash and went down to the sitting room. Mrs. Jowler heard him and appeared, beaming as usual, from the direction of the kitchen.

'Are you ready for your tea, sir?' she asked. 'I thought you might be having a rest so I didn't disturb you. The other gentleman has gone out.'

'I'd like some tea very much,' said

Lowe. 'Has my secretary been in?'

Mrs. Jowler shook her head.

'No, sir.'

She bustled away and Lowe want into the sitting room. Had Arnold White succeeded in discovering something? Judging from his non-appearance it looked as if he had.

Mrs. Jowler came in carrying a laden tray.

'I've made some scones,' she announced, 'and that's homemade strawberry jam.' She set the tray down on the table. 'If there's anything else you want p'raps you'd just call me?'

Trevor Lowe looked at the tea she had prepared and smiled.

'I shall never be able to eat a quarter of that,' he said.

'You eat as much you can, sir,' advised Mrs. Jowler. 'That's what you need on a holiday — lots of food an' plenty of rest.' She chuckled as she went out of the room and closed the door. Lowe poured himself out a cup of tea and helped himself to a scone. Both the scones and the jam were excellent. He ate two and drank a second cup of tea. He was very satisfied with his afternoon's work. He was pretty sure that his theory would prove to be correct. But he still had to discover what the Monk's Tomb meant.

He decided to stroll down to the village pub and see if he could pick up any information there. By the time he got there it would be open. He left a note for White telling him where he had gone and set off.

It was a beautiful evening and he enjoyed his walk along the quiet winding road.

At length he reached 'The Cheerful Abbot', Long Norton's only inn. The bar was not very full. It was too early yet. But there was a handful of locals drinking pints of beer and discussing the murder at Abbey Lodge.

The dramatist went up to the counter and ordered a double Haig. When it was brought to him by the pleasant-faced landlord and he had added a little water, he said, as he put down a pound note:

'I wonder if you could help me? I want to find a place somewhere round here called the Monk's Tomb. Have you ever heard of it?'

The landlord took the note in his large hands and his broad face puckered up into a thoughtful frown. After a pause he shook his head slowly.

'Can't say I 'ave, sir,' he replied. 'There's a lot o' things round these parts called friars an' abbots an' such like, on account o' the Abbey, but I ain't never 'eard o' the Monks Tomb.'

He sorted out the change for the pound and put it down on the counter.

'What sort o' place would it be, sir?' he asked.

Lowe drank part of his Haig.

'I don't know,' he said. 'I was hoping you would be able to tell me.'

'I'm afraid I can't, sir,' said the landlord. He went to serve a newcomer, and an old man who was sucking at an empty pipe between toothless gums, edged his way along the bar.

'Was you askin' fer the Monk's Tomb, sir?' he asked.

'That's right,' answered Lowe. 'Do you know it?'

The old man uttered a throaty little chuckle. He was a very old man. He wore an ancient cloth cap and carried a rough, blackthorn stick under his arm. His twinkling black eyes belied his age, which must have been in the region of ninety.

'There ain't much about these parts what I doesn't know,' answered the old man. 'Born an' bred in Long Norton, I was.'

He put down his empty tankard on the bar.

Lowe took the hint and called for it to be refilled.

When the old man had taken a long pull, Lowe said:

'Can you tell me what the Monk's Tomb is?'

'Aye, I can that,' said the old man, wiping his lips with the back of a gnarled hand. 'In the churchyard it be. Yer see the church were built where the old monastery used ter be.' He chuckled again. 'I don't s'pose 'alf a dozen folk 'ud be able ter tell yer about the Monk's Tomb,' he went on proudly, 'but I can. 'Cos why? 'Cos I uster ter play in that there churchyard when I was a lad, see?'

'Is it easy to find?' asked Lowe.

The old man shook his head.

'It ain't easy — not unless yer know where to look,' he replied. He took another swig at his beer. 'The part where it is ain't used now. Over by the wall what divides the churchyard from the grounds of Abbey Lodge, it be.'

Trevor Lowe thanked him. He felt a tinge of excitement. This place must be important or Berman wouldn't have noted it down. But what was it's importance?

The old man had launched into a rambling history of the village, and Lowe, although he answered in monosyllables, scarcely heard a word he was saying. As soon as he could, he finished his Haig, made an excuse to the old man, and left the inn.

He wanted to have a look at the Monk's Tomb without delay. As rapidly as he could he walked back the way he had came, and presently came to the entrance to the drive of Abbey Lodge. Passing this he continued on his way until he came to the lych gate that gave access to the churchyard.

By the time he reached it, the perspiration was streaming down his face and he had to wipe it away with his handkerchief. He passed through the gate and found himself in the churchyard, the more modern part of it.

Rows and rows of white tombstones, interspersed with monuments in marble and stone, lined the path on either side and stretched away among neatly trimmed grass. But the part he was seeking lay further on, where the trimmed grass frayed out into weeds and briars, overshadowed by trees, and only the moss-grown, crumbling stones at the head of a few forgotten graves reared up like the broken and decayed teeth in mouths of the aged.

Keeping in the shadow of the trees, for he had no wish to be seen by anyone who might be in the vicinity of the church, he made his way to the dividing wall that shut off the grounds of Abbey Lodge.

It took him quite a long time before he found the Monk's Tomb, but at last he came upon it. It was a huge, oblong slab of crumbling, lichen-covered granite, supported on all four sides by walls of the same material. On the top of the slab lay a recumbent figure that time and the action of the elements had reduced to shapelessness.

Lowe looked at the ancient mausoleum curiously. There was little doubt that this was what he sought. Carved on one of the walls was a half-obliterated inscription. He was able to pick out a word here and there.

'FRA . . . ..LECUS . . . .REQUIES-CAT IN PACE . . . 14 . . . '

The tomb was almost touching the wall of the Allerdyce estate, so close indeed that it was impossible to walk between. He had to content himself with an examination of the other three sides.

What was the secret of this ancient burial place?

Why had it interested Berman so much that he had noted it down? Was it a meeting place, or had it some deeper significance?

There was nothing extraordinary about

it except perhaps its age. And then he saw something . . .

It was a faint stain on the old stone, a stain that you would hardly expect to find there — oil!

He leaned forward and peered closer. There was no mistake, it was oil. But how came oil on this neglected grave of some long dead monk?

It was the merest smear, near a crack where two stone slabs joined. But when he touched it, it was still wet.

His pulse began to beat a shade faster. He felt that he was on the verge of an important discovery. People don't drop oil on an old tomb for nothing. There must be some very good reason for its presence. And it wasn't difficult to guess the reason . . .

Inch by inch he examined that end of the tomb. It was built rather like a huge, oblong box. The end where the oil had stained the stone was covered like the rest of the structure with a greenish-coloured deposit. Presently he made another discovery. At a point near the ground, hidden from view by the rank grass that grew in profusion round it, he found a small, projecting knob of stone from which the green deposit had been rubbed clean.

Was this the secret of the Monk's Tomb?

He was pretty certain that it was. There was only one conclusion to be drawn from the difference between the knob and the rest of the old burial place. The knob was clean because it had been constantly used!

Lowe looked round sharply. The churchyard was empty. There was nobody about. Carefully he reached down, pressing aside the grass that screened the projection, and pressed the knob.

Nothing happened!

It felt a little loose under his pressure but that was all. He tried pulling it. Still nothing happened.

Perhaps, after all, he had made a mistake.

He turned it to the left. It was immovable!

Rather irritably he gave it a twist in the opposite direction . . .

This time it shifted easily in nearly a half-circle. At the same time there was a loud click and the heavy slab of stone that formed that end of the tomb began to swing inwards, like a door. It opened about three inches and then stopped.

Lowe pushed firmly against it and it swung right back revealing the black interior of the vault. The projecting knob had evidently released a catch.

He took out his torch and shone a light into the dark void. Almost immediately inside was the top of a flight of worn stone steps that led downwards into darkness. What lay at the bottom of the steps?

Trevor Lowe was determined to find out before he was a minute older.

7

Arnold White opened his eyes.

At first he wondered vaguely where he was, and then he remembered!

The lethal chamber!

He must have fallen asleep after Greach and the other man had gone. It was quite dark. He couldn't see a thing. He had no idea of the time or how long he had slept. Not that it mattered much. What did matter was that he was in a dangerous position and the thing to do was to try and get out of it before it was too late.

But that was easier decided on than done.

He tried again to loosen the cords that bound his wrists. If he could get free . . . ?

But there was no better result than before. They had been tied too tightly. And his fingers weren't much use. They were so numbed that he could hardly feel anything, and his feet and legs were like lumps of lead.

He gave it up at last and lay still, breathless.

It seemed pretty hopeless. If he couldn't free himself there was precious little he could do.

There was just a chance that Trevor Lowe would come in search of him when he found that he had failed to come back to Mrs. Jowler's. But it was the barest possible chance. And even if he did, would he think of looking in the lethal chamber?

It was true that he was already suspicious of Greach and he had ordered White to watch the lethal chamber for the man he believed was hiding there.

But would he take action in time?

Arnold had no idea how late it was. If it was already dark outside, they might turn on the chloroform at any moment. After that it would only a matter of minutes.

He was quite helpless, trussed up like a chicken. He couldn't even shout. The gag was fastened too tightly for that.

It was a bleak prospect and he felt his courage ebbing away. But he realised that he'd got to grit his teeth and keep on hoping. To take his mind off the thought of the chloroform he forced himself to go over what had happened. Who was the man in the raincoat? Without doubt he was the guiding power in the whole business.

It might have been Glenister. He was the right build, but his voice had been so muffled by the handkerchief, or whatever it was that had covered his face, there was no clue to be got from that.

He wondered if they would come back before the end, but concluded that it was unlikely. This train of thought led him to speculate on how the chloroform was to be admitted from the outside tank. He remembered that there had been a pipe leading downwards which had entered the wall of the lethal chamber about a foot above ground level. Trevor Lowe had pointed this out. There had been a kind of stop-cock in the pipe . . .

A sudden thought struck him. If he could find the end of the inlet pipe where it entered the chamber it might be possible to block it in some way. The snag was that he couldn't use his hands, but perhaps he could free them sufficiently to use his fingers . . . ?

With the prospect of doing something, even though it was such a slender hope, his spirits rose. He began to work his fingers about to restore the circulation and get rid of the numbness. It was a very gradual business but presently he began to feel the prickling of pins and needles and his fingers felt less like lumps of dead flesh.

His hands had been tied behind his back and he had to roll over on his stomach. Continuing the treatment, he found after a while, that although he was still helpless, he could move his fingers about and even his hands a little.

He decided that he would have to have something with which to block up the inlet pipe, if and when he found it. He managed to get hold of the edge of his jacket and fumbled for the lining. If he could tear a strip off the lining it would supply him with what he needed.

It took him a long time to find the centre seam, longer still to get his fingernail in the seam and rip it open.

But he managed it and succeeded in tearing away a large piece of the silken lining. So far so good, he thought, as he recovered his breath from the effort. But the next part of the programme was infinitely the more difficult.

To find the small orifice of the pipe in that pitch blackness was almost, if not quite, impossible. But at least he could try and anything was better than just waiting.

He remembered that the tank had been in the right hand wall when he had seen it from outside. If he could find the iron door to the courtyard, he could take his bearings from that. There was no vestige of light round the edges to show where it was. It fitted too closely for that. But he knew that the other entrance, the one through which he had been brought from the tunnel, was somewhere behind him. That left three other sides in one of which the door must be.

He began to roll himself along the floor. It was quite a difficult job and he seemed to have been travelling a long way before he hit something solid.

One of the walls?

He turned round until he could feel it with his fingers.

And they touched iron!

By a stroke of luck he had found his objective first go off. The tank, then, must be on the left of this iron door. Its position inside would be the reverse of outside. His head was beginning to ache from his exertion, but he gritted his teeth and stuck at it.

This part was the hardest of all.

He had to edge himself along with his back to the wall, feeling inch by inch with his fingers for the tiny inlet. And there was always the chance that he would miss it. It seemed to him that hours must have passed before he found it.

It was so small that he could easily have missed, but his luck had held. Now, what he had to do was to block it up.

He was fumbling with a strip of the lining when he stopped and listened.

A faint sound had reached him from the other side of the chamber, the side containing the entrance through which he had been carried.

It was the sound of a footstep.

Arnold White held his breath.

Could it be Greach and the other man returning? His heart pounded in his chest. If so, all his efforts would have been in vain . . .

He could hear nothing now. And then there came the scrape of a key in a lock and a sharp click. This was followed by a gentle creaking sound. He felt a draught of cold, clammy air as the door was opened and then the light of a torch suddenly blazed through the darkness of the lethal chamber . . .

★   ★   ★

Trevor Lowe cautiously descended the first few steps, and paused.

It would be as well, he thought, to close the entrance before proceeding any further, in case anyone should stray into the churchyard while he was exploring below.

If there were no means of opening it again from the inside it would be distinctly awkward, but it was a risk that had to be taken. But there must be some way of working the opening from within. He examined the spot where the heavy stone slab shut, standing on three of the steps down, and discovered to his satisfaction that there was, on the inside, an iron projection that corresponded with the stone knob outside. It evidently worked on the same principle. Closing the slab, he tried it, and found that it opened easily when he turned the rusty iron lever.

There was nothing to worry about there. He shut the slab and continued to descend the steps. It was very damp inside the tomb and the steps were covered with a film of slime. He had to go carefully, in consequence, for fear of slipping.

Keeping the light of his torch on the steps he went carefully down. The smell of damp and decay grew stronger the further he descended. Patches of fungi spread over the walls and the entire place was dripping with moisture.

The odour of the place was like the

odour of death itself, cold as the clasp of dead fingers. It was cold too, a clammy cold, that made him shiver as he went lower and lower.

The steps ended at last and he found that he was standing in a square, cell-like room that had apparently been hewn out of solid rock. There were ledges on either wall on which rested rough stone coffins. They were covered in the slimy deposit that seemed to ooze from everywhere. He concluded that this was the burial place of the old monks and the coffins contained their remains.

It was an unpleasant place. In the corners were piles of heaped up debris from which yellow bones projected and from one of which a skull peered out, its eyeless sockets seeming to wink in the shifting light of the torch.

A hidden graveyard, buried in the depths of the earth. A terrifying place of long dead men.

In one of the walls was an arched doorway. He went over to this and peered through, shining his torch into the darkness beyond. Passing through the arch, he looked about him.

Here was another vault, similar to the first, with shelves filled with more coffins. The whole place was redolent of death and decay.

There was one notable difference.

In the centre of the floor was a huge stone tomb, almost an exact copy of the one above. Trevor Lowe saw that one. of the ends gaped open, revealing a black aperture inside. The light of his torch showed him that whatever had once been inside the second tomb had now gone. There were more steps leading down but he found that there were not nearly so many as before.

At the bottom of the steps was a passage that led away into more darkness. It was narrow and the roof was low. The stone floor was broken and there were a number of pools of stagnant water. The air was foul and heavy and he was forced to go carefully because the passage twisted sharply in a series of unexpected turns.

He had to stoop to avoid hitting his head on the roof as he went gingerly along, and to his surprise the air began to get better. Somewhere ahead there must be some kind of an outlet to account for this. Perhaps there was a ventilation shaft communicating with the outside air.

The passage seemed never ending. The moisture dripped from the roof and the fungi grew in huge, bloated-looking patches on the walls and between the broken stones of the floor.

The whole place must have been a good way underground. He wondered as he moved slowly along what it had originally been? And where did it lead to?

For one thing he was thankful. There appeared to be no rats. In most places of this kind they were to be found in swarms but he had seen nothing of the kind.

Presently the passage dipped sharply. A pool of water over a foot deep had accumulated in the depression and he had to wade through it, but on the other side the tunnel began to ascend again.

Surely, thought Lowe, it can't go on much further? He must have come a considerable distance from the church-yard already. But the passage went on for another fifty yards or so before it took a sharp bend to the right and began to widen considerably. Ahead he saw that there was another archway and when he reached this, he discovered that beyond was a third vault-like room, but with a very great difference.

It was much larger than the other two and there were no coffin-filled shelves on the walls. It was free, too, from the dust and debris that had filled the others. But the thing that amazed him as he flashed the torch from side to was that it was furnished!

And very curiously furnished too!

A large table stood in the centre on a square of carpet. And the table was covered with a cloth of black velvet on which stood a green-shaded reading lamp. Drawn up by the table was a comfortable swivel chair of the kind to be found in offices. But the most incongruous object of all was the huge, green-painted safe that stood against one wall!

Trevor Lowe examined the place carefully. The lamp was a powerful one, burning petrol-vapour, and appeared to be the only means of lighting this queer underground office. The safe was a very large one of modern make, a small strongroom.

How it had ever been brought into this chamber was a mystery. But there was no mystery concerning the use of this hidden room.

This must be the headquarters of the diamond bandit!

This was where the stolen diamonds were brought and sorted. That was the explanation of the safe.

On the thick velvet pile of the table covering, beside the lamp, lay a powerful magnifying glass. There was little room for doubt. This was where the stones were examined and afterwards transferred to the safe.

Lowe made a closer examination of the safe. It was a combination safe, thief-resisting and fireproof. He could picture the diamond thief sitting at that table examining his latest haul under the powerful light of the vapour-lamp, and exulting as the stones flashed and sparkled on their ebon bed.

And he thought he could put a name to the person who was in the habit of sitting there.

But before he could pass his theory on to Shadgold he would have to find substantial evidence to support it. He had nothing to corroborate his idea.

In the meanwhile, he still had to find out the ultimate end of the underground passage. This chamber merely formed a kind of junction in it, as the others had.

Facing the archway by which he had entered this underground sanctum was another, and beyond it, the passage apparently continued. He could return and give the office-chamber a closer examination later.

He started on a further exploration. This part of the tunnel was larger and higher than the preceding part. It shelved upwards at a steep angle.

That meant that it must be returning to the surface. It shouldn't be long now before he came to the other exit, if there was one. And he was right. A few yards of the tunnel and he came to the foot of another flight of stone steps. They were quite short and he could see that at the top of them was what looked like a wooden door.

He went up the steps and tried the door. It was locked. Perhaps there was a key kept near. It was more than likely if this door was used much, and he imagined that this was probably the way that the diamond thief came to his underground room. He would hardly use the Monk's Tomb entrance with that long tortuous passage to negotiate. This was much easier and nearer.

He searched about and at first he could see nothing of the sort. Perhaps he was mistaken. Perhaps the bandit kept the key on him. But just in case of forgetfulness, surely there should be a spare . . .

And then he found it, hidden in a corner of the steps. It hadn't been used for a long time, because the dampness of the place had covered it with rust.

It took him some time to insert it in the lock and turn it. The rust made it stiff and when he did turn it, it rasped.

But when he turned the handle the door opened with a faint creak. A smell of stale apples wafted out to his nostrils, a sickly odour that enveloped him like a chiffon veil.

As the door opened wider he saw that beyond was utter darkness. He paused, listening, before risking putting on his torch.

But everything was still, there was not a sound.

He switched on his light and stepped into the room. And as the odour grew stronger, he realised where he was.

The end of the passage from the Monk's Tomb in the churchyard led straight into the lethal chamber, and the sickly odour was the odour of chloroform!

8

It was a significant discovery. Trevor Lowe wondered how many people in the household of Abbey Lodge were aware of its existence.

Standing in the doorway he allowed his light to play backwards and forwards over the chamber in front of him.

And then he uttered a startled exclamation.

Something was lying huddled against one wall. Surely he hadn't discovered another tragedy? Keeping the light on the object, he advanced swiftly. One glance at the light grey suit and his heart jumped.

It was Arnold!

He dropped quickly on one knee, dreading what he would find. A wave of relief swept over him as he saw that his secretary's eyes were open and staring at him with a mingled expression of wonderment and delight.

Trevor Lowe swiftly unfastened the

gag, took his pocketknife from his pocket, and slashed through the cords at his wrists and ankles.

It was some time before White could speak. His lips and tongue were dry and swollen. All he could utter was a hoarse croak.

'Take it easy,' said Lowe. He began to rub the numbed and useless legs and arms of his secretary to try and restore the circulation.

Arnold White swallowed hard.

'How did you get here?' he asked almost inaudibly.

The dramatist told him briefly while he continued the massage. Arnold winced with pain as the blood began to flow back through his veins, but he could move his limbs a little.

'Now it's your turn,' said Lowe. 'How did you get in this mess?'

With his voice growing stronger every minute, Arnold jerkily recounted what had happened to him. By the time he had finished, he was able to stagger unsteadily to his feet with Lowe's help.

'We'd better get out of here as quickly

as possible,' said the dramatist. 'How do you feel?'

'I'm all right now,' muttered White. 'I could do with a drink, though. My mouth and throat feel like sandpaper.'

'I'm afraid you'll have to wait for that,' said his employer. 'We've got quite a way to go. Now, catch hold of my arm.'

He led the way to the door, helped Arnold through, and then shut and locked the door, pocketing the key.

'We may need that,' he grunted.

Gingerly, Arnold White made his way down the steps. His legs were weak and shaky but they got stronger as he continued to use them.

He looked with amazement as they came to the office-chamber, but Lowe cut short his stammered questions. There was no time to explain any more just then. That could come later when they reached Mrs. Jowler's, and his secretary had been fed and given something to drink.

It was dusk when they emerged from the Monk's Tomb in the churchyard. White drew in the fresh air gratefully. The fumes with which the lethal chamber had been impregnated had given him a headache and made him feel dizzy. But the clean, sweet air soon cleared away these effects, and they set off as quickly as possible for the cottage.

When they reached it they found Detective-Inspector Shadgold ensconced in the sitting room enjoying a large John Haig.

'Hello,' he greeted as they came in, 'where have you two been? I helped myself to a drink, I hope . . . ' He broke off and eyed them keenly. 'What's the matter?' he went on. 'You look as if you'd been having a rough time.'

'White has,' answered Lowe. He rang the bell. 'Now,' he continued. 'You're going to have a stiff whisky and a meal and then you're going to bed.'

He picked up the bottle of Haig, poured out a good portion, added some water, and gave it to his secretary.

'Drink that,' he said, 'it'll put you right in no time.'

Mrs. Jowler appeared in answer to his ring and he explained to her that White had eaten nothing since breakfast but without saying why.

The landlady was horrified.

'My goodness!' she exclaimed, 'You must be starving! I'll bring you a lovely meal in a few minutes. I've got a nice piece of steak with some mushrooms and potatoes. It won't take long.'

She gave White a beaming smile and bustled away.

'Now,' grunted Shadgold, 'perhaps you'll do a bit of explaining? You look as if you'd been down a sewer.'

'That's not a bad description,' retorted Trevor Lowe. He poured himself out a Haig. 'You'd never guess where I have been. That horse of Berman's was a winner!'

'Horse? What the deuce . . . Oh, you mean Monk's Tomb? Did you find out what it is?'

'I certainly did. You're going to get a surprise when I tell you,' answered Lowe.

'Well, hurry up and get on with it,' said the inspector. 'I need something to counteract Bracken . . . '

'Been difficult, has he?'

Shadgold snorted.

'He's a pig-headed idiot!' he said. 'But I'll tell you about him later. I want to hear what you've been up to.'

Lowe told him. He was interrupted by the arrival of Mrs. Jowler with a laden tray, which she set before White.

'I'll bring you some tea,' she said, 'after I bring you your cherry pie.'

Arnold White thanked her and set to work on the meal, while Lowe continued his story.

The inspector was excited.

'By the lord Harry!' he cried when the dramatist had finished. 'This is conclusive. We've got enough on Greach to pull him, in at once . . .'

'It would be a bad move,' interrupted Lowe, shaking his head. 'We might get him to talk but I doubt it . . .'

'But they're bound to find out that White's gone,' said Shadgold. 'They'll smell a rat. They may even try and make a getaway.'

'I doubt if the diamond thief will,' said Lowe.

'And that's Glenister,' put in Shadgold.

164

'Well, we shall see,' said his friend. 'I have a plan which I think will succeed.'

Shadgold opened his mouth to ask what it was, but Lowe gave him a warning frown and glanced in White's direction.

'What trouble have you been having with Bracken?' he asked to change the subject.

'Well,' explained the inspector, 'I was feeling a bit of a nit keeping what I know to myself. After all, although I don't like the chap, he is in charge of the murder case and it was really my duty to give him any information I could . . . '

'You told him about the Spander, eh?'

Shadgold nodded.

'Yes,' he grunted. 'He was most offensive. He declared that I should have told him at once. He wanted to go off there and then and arrest Glenister.'

'I'm glad you persuaded him not to,' said Lowe.

'I had a job,' retorted Shadgold. 'I had to threaten that if he did, I'd get on to the Yard and make a complaint that he was interfering with me in the course of my duty. Of course, I don't know that it would have cut a lot of ice — these locals can pretty well do as they like, you know, but it worked! He calmed down a bit and agreed to wait.'

'He won't have to wait very long,' said the dramatist. 'We'll have the whole thing tied up and done with sooner than you expect.'

Shadgold made a grimace.

'Well, I hope you know what you're doing,' he said. 'I think we should pull in Greach straight away . . . '

'We'll deal with Greach, don't worry,' broke in the dramatist.

Mrs. Jowler brought in the cherry pie and a large pot of tea. When Arnold White had finished the pie and had drank two cups of tea, Trevor Lowe packed him off to bed.

'Now,' he said, when the secretary had gone, 'we can get down to business . . . '

'What's the idea of not talking in front of young White?' asked Shadgold. 'He's safe enough . . . '

'Oh, he's safe enough,' interrupted Lowe, 'but he'd have wanted to come and he's had enough for one day.'

'Come where?' demanded the inspector.

Trevor Lowe picked up the bottle of Haig and poured out two stiff drinks. One he handed to Shadgold.

'Drink that while I tell you,' he said. 'You may need it before the night's over.'

★ ★ ★

The moon had not yet risen when Trevor Lowe and Shadgold left Mrs. Jowler's and started to walk briskly towards the churchyard.

The inspector was unusually silent. He did not altogether approve of the dramatist's plan, but from past experience he was willing to fall in with Lowe's suggestions. They had invariably proved right.

The night wasn't dark. That twilight which persists for so long on a fine summer evening still lingered, giving the sky a bluish-green tinge that was rapidly growing deeper. There was no wind and everything was very still when they reached the churchyard. The village of Long Norton went to bed early for it was awake with the lark, and they were the only visible people abroad.

Lowe led Shadgold over to the Monk's Tomb and showed him how the mechanism worked.

'We shall have to be careful,' he warned, as he began to descend the stone steps. 'This place is frequently used and we don't want to run foul of the person who uses it — yet.'

Shadgold grunted.

'I can't see why we couldn't go after Greach at his home,' he said. 'That would have . . . '

'We may kill two birds with one stone, this way,' said Lowe. 'They will come to remove the body of White from the lethal chamber, and we can catch them red-handed. The only danger is that they've already found out that he isn't there, but I don't think they'll make a move until much later . . . '

'And if they have?' asked the inspector.

'Then we can go after Greach at his home,' said Lowe. 'Now, don't talk any more. Sound travels easily in a place like this.'

They were both armed with torches and Shadgold was interested when they reached the first vault with its stone shelves and coffins. But Lowe hurried him on, through the second vault, and on until they came to the office-chamber.

Shadgold stared at the table, the lamp, and the big safe. Although he had been prepared what to expect from the description Lowe had already given him, the place surprised him.

But he had no time to examine it very closely. Lowe gripped his arm when he would have lingered and pulled him through the arch into the last section of the passage.

They splashed their way through the stagnant water and eventually reached the steps that led up to the door opening into the lethal chamber.

Here, Lowe paused, and putting his lips close to Shadgold's ear he said, in a whisper;

'I imagine they will come to remove White by the other entrance. If there's any sign of chloroform in the place we shall have to come back here. Keep your handkerchief over your nose and mouth when I open this door.'

Shadgold nodded.

The dramatist took the key from his pocket and put it in the lock. Before leaving the cottage he had wiped it free of the encrusted rust and given it a spot of oil so that this time it turned more easily. A strong smell of chloroform came gushing out, and he closed it again quickly.

The sickly odour flooded the confined space at, the top of the steps.

'They must've turned the stuff on already,' he whispered to Shadgold. 'The lethal chamber is flooded with it.'

'Which means that we're too late,' the inspector whispered back.

'I don't think so.' Lowe's voice was barely audible. 'They'll wait until it's safe for them to go in, I should think. We can hear when they open the iron door.'

He descended a few steps and sat down. The pungent smell of the drug was still strong but it was dispersing.

Shadgold perched himself on one of the steps just below the dramatist and sighed.

Why did Lowe always have to take the most dramatic course? It would have been so much simpler to have pulled Greach in. White could have identified him, and he could have been held on a charge of assault. Easy! Instead of which, here they were, stuck in this unpleasant passage, and quite possibly likely to have to stay for a long time.

The time passed slowly without the faintest sound from behind the closed door to the lethal chamber. Perhaps, thought the inspector, they wouldn't come at all that night. They might wait until the following night. If they thought that the chloroform had done its work and Arnold White was dead, what was the hurry in removing the body? It was safe enough in the lethal chamber. So far as they knew nobody was likely to search the place.

He looked at his watch. The luminous dial showed that it was well past eleven — nearing the half-hour, as a matter of fact — and Shadgold found the step he was sitting on both damp and remarkably hard. How much longer would they have to keep this uncomfortable vigil?

Half an hour passed and still there was no sound from the lethal chamber. Shadgold shifted uneasily as the sharp edge of the step against which he was leaning cut into his back.

'How much longer do we have to hang about here?' he whispered.

'I don't know,' answered Lowe. 'I may have made a miscalculation.' Shadgold felt him move in the darkness. 'I'm going to have another look inside the chamber.'

He got to his feet and moved up the steps. He had not locked the door and he cautiously opened it. The fumes from the chloroform were still strong. He put on the torch and swept the light round the dark interior of the lethal chamber.

And then he drew in his breath sharply.

Something was lying on the floor near the iron door . . .

Covering his mouth with his handkerchief and holding his breath, Lowe stepped quickly across the floor to the huddled form by the door.

It was the body of a man, lying on his face, his arms flung out before his head. Trevor Lowe bent down and turned the man over so that he could see his face.

It was Greach!

He was dead and he had not died from the effects of the chloroform. The front of his shirt was wet with blood and there was a small hole in the cloth.

Greach had been shot!

'I should have expected this to happen,' said Lowe when he had told Shadgold. 'We can't go in there yet. The fumes are still too strong . . . '

'But I don't understand,' began the inspector. 'Who shot him? Why . . . ?'

'Because White had seen Greach and must have recognised him,' answered Lowe. 'They must've come back earlier than I expected — before we got here — to remove the body. When they found White had gone it was obvious that he had either escaped or been rescued. That signed Greach's death warrant. The diamond bandit wasn't risking the fact that the man might talk when he was arrested . . . '

'And that's what we should have done,' broke in Shadgold. 'You can't say I didn't suggest it . . .'

'I'm not trying to,' snapped the dramatist. 'It was my fault, and I'm willing to take the blame.'

'In the meanwhile, what do we do?' asked the inspector. 'Greach's murder should be notified at once . . .'

'If you do that,' said Lowe, 'you'll have to reveal that we know about this passage leading from the tomb to the lethal chamber, which also means that we know about the office-chamber . . .'

'Well?' interposed Shadgold.

'In that case our best chance of catching our man goes west,' said the dramatist.

'We can't just leave the body in there and say nothing,' grunted the inspector. 'I could get into serious trouble . . .'

'There's a way out of that,' interrupted Lowe. 'You must find an excuse for searching the lethal chamber from the courtyard entrance. This door can leave locked. We've got to keep our knowledge of the passage to ourselves for a little while longer. I'll lock the door now, and we can go back the way we came.'

Shadgold was reluctant but he saw the force of the dramatist's argument about the passage. Lowe locked the door to the lethal chamber and they began to make their way back to the churchyard.

When they reached the furnished room, the inspector suggested that they might examine the place more closely. Lowe agreed.

While Shadgold was looking at the safe, he lifted the velvet cloth that draped the table. As he had expected there was a drawer in the front of it, and pulling this open, he found that it contained two slim red-covered books, like school exercise books.

'How the dickens anybody ever got that safe down here, I don't know,' said Shadgold. 'Hello, what have you found?'

'I don't know. I found them in the drawer.' Lowe opened the first one and in the light of the torch they bent over it.

It contained a list of names in a neat hand.

'Great Scott!' exclaimed Shadgold, peering down at the list. 'These are some of the worst lot of characters you could find in a day's march. Most of 'em are in C.R.O at the Yard . . . '

'There's Berman among them,' Lowe pointed to the name. 'These must be some of the people he's used to help him. Let's see what else there is.'

He turned the pages rapidly. There was nothing more in it until he came to the last page. Here the list of names was repeated but by the side of each were dates and figures.

This puzzled him for a moment, then he understood.

The dates represented when that particular person had been used for a robbery, the figures were the amount he had been paid. He explained this to the inspector.

'Very methodical,' grunted Shadgold. 'What's in the other book?'

This proved to be even more interesting for it contained a complete description of every piece of jewellery that the diamond thief had stolen.

'Well, these two books are pretty damning!' said the inspector. 'Once we've got our man . . . '

'Quiet!' whispered Lowe suddenly.

He switched out the torch and listened. A sound had come from the direction of the passage leading to the Monk's Tomb. It was faint but his ears had caught it, the chink of a foot on stone.

Someone had entered the passage by the Monk's Tomb!

Shadgold had heard the faint sound, which was now more distinct as the person, whoever it was, drew nearer. Lowe took the inspector by the arm and drew him into the archway leading to the lethal chamber. Here they waited in utter darkness while footsteps drew nearer.

They were completely hidden from anyone who entered the vault by the rough buttress that supported the arch.

The sound of the approaching footsteps grew louder and louder. They heard a muttered oath as the newcomer stumbled, and presently a faint glimmer of light appeared in the darkness beyond the other archway.

The light became brighter and they saw that it was a torch. Presently the vague shape of a man came through the archway into the vault.

He paused just within the arch and flashed his light from side to side. Lowe saw that he carried some heavy object. This he put down by the table in the centre and switched off his torch. For a second or two the place was dark again and then there came the scraping of a match. A flood of white light illuminated the vault as the newcomer lit the vapour-lamp.

In the brilliant light they saw who it was who had come there, and Shadgold drew in his breath with a little hiss.

The man was Berman!

It was the last person Lowe had expected. He had been prepared for someone quite different.

Watching, scarcely daring to breathe in case they should be heard; they saw 'Black' Berman pick up the object he had put down on the floor and carry it over to the safe.

It was a large and apparently heavy

suitcase. When he had taken it over to the safe; he came back and removed the green shade from the lamp so that the light shone all over the vault instead of being concentrated down on the table.

Then he took from the pocket of his jacket a stubby automatic, which he examined carefully, ensuring that a cartridge was in the breech.

After listening intently for a moment, he carried the lamp over to the safe, stood it on the floor, and put the automatic beside it. And then he began a close scrutiny of the safe. Closely and carefully he examined the lock and the dial of the combination.

Apparently satisfied, he straightened up, listened again, and then opened the suitcase.

From it he took what appeared to be a pair of wireless headphones, attached by long thin wires to a small round black disc.

He took off the cap he was wearing and adjusted the headphones over his ears. Next he put the round black disc against the door of the safe near the lock and pressed it lightly. It was evidently fitted with a sucker for it adhered to the shiny surface.

There was no mistaking the reason for Berman's presence there. He was going to attempt to open the safe! The microphone attachment was so that he could hear the tumblers drop as he gently turned the dial and so learn the combination. It was a method that had been used satisfactorily by skilled 'peter-men'. But Berman was not a skilled safebreaker. His line was blackmail, hence his nickname.

No doubt the enormous value of the contents of the safe had attracted him. There was no doubt in Trevor Lowe's mind that the safe held a fortune in diamonds, the entire proceeds of the diamond thief's various hauls.

He felt Shadgold's hand on his arm contract as the inspector watched Berman set to work methodically, slowly turning the dial while he listened for the slight sound in the headphones that would tell him each letter of the combination as he found it. So engrossed were Lowe and Shadgold that they forgot the passing of time, and the minutes flew by unheeded.

It took Berman over half an hour before, with a little grunt of satisfaction, he grasped the brass handle of the safe, turned it, and pulled the heavy door open.

In their interest and excitement neither Shadgold nor the dramatist became aware of the figure that loomed up behind them. The first warning came to Shadgold when he heard something swish and an agonizing pain shot through his head. Trevor Lowe swung round as the inspector fell, but he was too late. The cosh rose quickly and fell again . . .

As his senses fled Lowe heard the sound of a shot . . .

9

Although Arnold White had gone meekly up to bed when he was told, he had not the slightest intention of staying there.

He guessed that his employer and Shadgold would be up to something and he wasn't going to miss any excitement that might be going!

After all, he considered that he'd earned it.

So, as soon as he heard them leave the cottage, he crept down the stairs and followed. Now, all would have been well if he hadn't lost them. But he had given them too long a start while he hastily dressed, and there was no sign of them anywhere to be seen.

And he had no idea where they were going.

Perhaps it was their intention to keep a watch on the lethal chamber to catch Greach when he came to turn on the tap. Yes, that was probably what they would do. Well, there was no reason why he shouldn't be there too!

He felt completely recovered from his ordeal. Mrs. Jowler's excellent meal had done the trick. He wasn't going to be tucked away in bed while there was anything interesting likely to happen.

Keeping a careful look out so as not to run into Lowe or Shadgold unexpectedly, he made his way from the cottage to Abbey Lodge. Instead of walking up the drive he kept to the trees that lined it. Presently he found himself in the kitchen garden and within sight of the courtyard containing the kennels and the lethal chamber.

Now was the time for extreme caution. If Lowe and the inspector had come to watch the place they must be somewhere near. It would be fatal if he stumbled on them by accident.

But there was no sign of them!

He found the clump of laurel bushes where he had concealed himself earlier that day but it was empty. In its shelter, he sat down to think. It was obvious that he had made a mistake in believing that they had been coming here. Perhaps they had gone to the Monk's Tomb?

That was probable. Should he go there?

No, he wouldn't. There was apparently no one keeping an eye on the lethal chamber from this end. Something vital might occur and it would be nice to score one up on Lowe and Shadgold. Teach them to try and keep him out of things . . .

But nothing did.

A sliver of moon came up but it gave very little light, and he was just getting fed up with lurking in the laurels when he suddenly saw a tall figure appear in the kitchen garden.

Arnold caught his breath. Something was going to happen at last!

He couldn't see who it was, except that it was a man, but he seemed to be making for the drive. There was something furtive about his movements, however, that assured White that he wasn't just out for an evening stroll.

He made up his mind to follow the man, whoever he was. He wriggled his way out from the shelter of the bushes and got to his feet just as the man disappeared among the shrubbery that divided the kitchen garden from the drive.

Silently, Arnold White followed in his wake. The man paused when he reached the end of the straggling belt of trees that bordered the drive, and looked swiftly about him. Satisfied that there was no one about, he continued on his way.

As he emerged from the shadow of the trees, White was able to get a clearer view of him.

It was Captain Glenister!

He was dressed in a dinner jacket with a dark silk scarf wound round his neck. It covered the whiteness of his collar and shirt front.

Arnold felt that he was on the verge of a discovery. Where was Glenister going? If he had only come out for a breath of air, he wouldn't be behaving in this furtive manner. He expected him to turn in the direction of the main gate when he reached the drive. But he did nothing of the kind.

Still looking sharply about, Glenister

crossed the broad gravel stretch of the drive and plunged in among the trees on the other side.

White was disconcerted. If he followed the man he would have to cross that open stretch of gravel. If Glenister should look back, he couldn't fail to see him. However, it either meant risking it or losing him altogether. He decided to risk it.

He waited for what he judged would be time enough to allow Glenister to get well ahead, then, crouching down as low as he could in order to minimize the chance of being seen, he ran quickly across the gravel drive to the shelter of the copse on the other side.

He could no longer see the man he was following. He stopped for a moment behind a tree trunk and listened. Faintly he could hear the crackling of breaking twigs ahead.

He set off in the direction of the sound and presently he was able to gain a vague glimpse of Glenister moving through the trees.

He was taking a twisting path, and

Arnold puzzled his brains to think where the man could be making for. Was it possible that this was only an evening stroll after all? Surely no one would behave in that odd, furtive manner if that were all there was to it? There *must* be more. But where the deuce *could* Glenister be going?

It was with a sudden shock of surprise that he found out!

Quite unexpectedly there loomed up in front a high stone wall and beyond this, dimly outlined against the thin, crescent of the moon, the picturesque pile of the old church.

And Arnold White knew instantly where Glenister was making for! This was the boundary wall that separated the grounds of Abbey Lodge from the churchyard.

Glenister was going to the Monk's Tomb!

Arnold felt a wave of excitement flood over him. He hadn't been wasting his time after all. At least it proved that Glenister knew all about the passage that ran to the lethal chamber. And if he knew that, he must know about the office-room, the safe, and the rest of it . . .

Of course, he knew!

He was the diamond bandit!

As he watched, Glenister stopped, gave a slight spring and caught the top of the wall with his hands. A moment later he had pulled himself astride the coping and dropped into the churchyard.

Arnold, his heart beating rapidly, hurried along the wall until he was fifty yards from the place where Glenister had climbed over, and then he, too, did the same thing. As he slipped down into the churchyard, he looked toward the tomb and was just in time to see the slab guarding the entrance to the passage close. Glenister had descended into the tunnel.

White began to think rapidly. What should he do now? Stay where he was or follow Glenister?

He wondered where Trevor Lowe and Shadgold had got to. Had they gone down into the passage?

He made up his mind to go after Glenister. It would be risky but his curiosity was at fever heat. He made his way through the tall, rank grass to the tomb. He would have to give Glenister ample time to get a good way ahead before he ventured to follow.

Sound carried a long way in a place like that and he would have to move very carefully. In order that he could leave the cottage without disturbing Mrs. Jowler, he had put on a pair of crepe-soled shoes and he was glad that he had. They would make little sound on the stone floor of the passage. The danger would be in kicking any of the loose pieces of stone and rock that lay about. He would go gingerly.

He stooped, groped for the stone knob, and twisted it as he been shown by Lowe. With the faintest click the heavy slab moved back. Arnold pushed it fully open and felt his way partly down the stone steps. Re-closing the slab, he listened.

He could hear the faintest of sounds from far away. Cautiously, he moved down the steps. He had to do without any light. That would have been fatal, and he found that it was not easy to find his way in the dark — a darkness that felt almost solid. But by keeping one hand on the wall he managed to guide himself safely down the steps and along the first part of the passage. It was slow going. He had to test every step in case he sent any loose rubble rolling about.

Finding his way through the two coffin-vaults was even more difficult. Three times he nearly met with an accident, once when he blundered into the sharp corner of a stone shelf and banged his nose, and twice when he almost twisted his ankle in cracks in the uneven floor.

But he managed somehow to cover a good part of the way, and then he saw ahead a glimmer of light. It was brighter than a torch. Glenister must have reached the office-chamber and lighted the vapour-lamp.

Arnold decided that he would have to be careful now. But the light was a help . . .

And then, shattering the silence like a clap of thunder, came the sound of a shot!

He stopped dead, his heart jumping.

What had happened? Had Glenister run into Lowe and Shadgold?

Alarmed and now heedless of what noise he made, Arnold White hurried forward, stumbling over the rough ground and bumping against the sides of the narrow passage.

He could hear nothing but the light grew brighter as he neared the rough archway forming the entrance to the furnished vault.

And as he saw within, he pulled up with an exclamation of amazement.

It was a scene that was to live long in his memory!

The big vault was bright with the white light from the vapour-lamp, which stood on the floor by the big safe. Near it sprawled the body of a man with blood oozing from under him, one hand clawing out toward an automatic pistol that lay just out of reach.

Locked in each other's arms, swaying back and forth in a desperate struggle, were Glenister and the man in the raincoat. Glenister had the other man by the wrist and was straining to prevent him from turning an automatic he held against him.

Arnold took in the scene in a flash. With a bound he was across the vault and had snatched up the automatic from the floor by the dead man's hand.

'Hi, there!' he cried loudly. 'Break away and stick up your hands!'

But they never even heard him!

'Break away!' shouted Arnold. 'Do you hear me? If you don't break away I'll shoot!'

He stepped forward, gripped the automatic that the unknown was trying to turn on Glenister, and wrenched it from his hand.

They separated. Glenister looked at him in vague surprise, breathing hard from his recent struggle. The other man muttered an animal snarl and turned on him.

'Keep still, both of you!' snapped White, covering them steadily with an automatic in each hand. 'Put your hands over your head. If you try to move I'll shoot!'

The man in the raincoat, his face still

covered by the white cloth, crouched as though about to spring.

'I mean what I say!' cried Arnold, and made a gesture with the right hand automatic. The other uttered a thin, cackling little chuckle, and raised his hands.

'You needn't worry about me,' muttered Glenister quickly. 'I'm not in this . . . '

'I don't know what you're in, or what you're not in, but you'd better do what you're told.'

Glenister's face flushed. He looked as though he were going to make an angry retort but he thought better of it. With a slight shrug of his shoulders he put his arms up.

'That's better,' snapped Arnold White. 'Now get over there against the wall!'

They hesitated.

'Go on — both of you!'

Slowly then backed until they reached the blank wall of the vault behind them. Arnold stood watching them. So far so good, he thought. But what did he do next? At the moment he held the whip hand but if he relaxed his attention for a second it would give them a chance. He couldn't deal with both of them at once.

The man in the raincoat gave a little chuckle.

'Look here,' said Glenister steadily. 'You're Mr. Lowe's secretary, aren't you? I don't know what you're doing in this place, but you are making a mistake. If you'll let me I'll help you . . . '

'Nothing doing,' said Arnold.

'I give you my word,' said Glenister, 'that I have nothing to do with this business . . . '

'That's right, Arnold,' broke in the voice of Trevor Lowe rather shakily. 'Glenister's all right . . . '

Arnold, startled, looked round. The dramatist, white and shaking, appeared unsteadily from the archway. There was a large bruise on his forehead. He came forward and took one of the automatics from his secretary's hand. But while White's attention was distracted, the man in the raincoat acted.

With a howl of rage he hurled himself on the secretary and flung him to the ground. His hands clawed for his throat and it took the combined efforts of Lowe and Glenister to pull him off. He seemed possessed of superhuman strength. He fought desperately to try and tear himself from their grasp. And then suddenly his rage left him abruptly. They felt him sag limply between them,

Anticipating that it was a trick, Lowe took a firmer grip of his arm, and keeping the automatic pressed into his side, led him over to the swivel chair by the table. Into this he collapsed, huddling himself up with his chin on his breast.

Arnold White got to his feet unsteadily and fingered his bruised throat.

'Gosh!' he said huskily. 'A little of that goes a long way . . . '

He picked up the automatic that had fallen from his hand.

'Who is it?' he asked.

Trevor Lowe leaned over the man in the chair and pulled off the white covering from his face. White gave an exclamation of surprise as he saw the distorted face.

'Doctor Allerdyce!' he cried.

Lowe shook his head.

'Not *Doctor* Allerdyce,' he corrected. 'Sir Reginald.'

Glenister shot him a quick glance.

'So you know that?' he said.

Lowe nodded.

'You've known it all along, haven't you?' he said.

'No, I didn't know it until after the shooting of Superintendent Drincott,' answered Glenister.

'But,' interrupted Arnold, 'Sir Reginald was killed.'

'Doctor Allerdyce was killed,' said Trevor Lowe. 'He was killed by his brother . . . '

The man in the chair gave a little chuckle of laughter.

'I killed him,' he declared. 'I killed him! And I'd kill him again to keep my beautiful diamonds.' He peered round over his shoulder. 'As I killed that swine there! He was going to rob me of my beautiful stones, my lovely glittering diamonds that I've collected for so long. But no one shall take them away. They are mine!' He uttered another little chuckle of laughter, and White realised that he was mad!

'Yes, yes,' went on the other, nodding rapidly and speaking in a low tone as though he were talking to himself, 'I killed him. He discovered my secret . . . He saw me looking at the ring that night in my study and he recognised it from the description in the newspapers. He threatened to expose me. He's been prying on me for a long time. He wanted to find out where I went at nights. He never found this place, though.' A look of sly cunning crept into his eyes. 'Nobody knew that I came here to look at my beautiful diamonds . . . Watching them glint and shine and sparkle like living drops of white-hot fire . . . I lived for them, my lovely stones . . . '

He was almost crooning and a thin white froth appeared on his lips. White looked at him with something like horror in his eyes. This witless thing that had been a man . . .

'I used to let them trickle through my fingers,' went on the madman, oblivious it seemed of their presence, 'cool and full of shooting colours — imprisoned rainbows in ice. He wanted me to give them back!' His voice rose to a scream. 'To give them back to the stupid people who never appreciated their beauty. I killed him! I stabbed him with the paper knife on my desk . . . ' He made a motion with his hand of striking. 'After I'd done it, I was frightened — horribly frightened! If I was found out I should be locked up and my diamonds taken from me. But I kept cool. Geoffrey used to tell me I was unbalanced, but I'm not. I was clever. I changed places with Geoffrey. It would be me they found in the morning, not him.'

He stopped and turned his eyes on Glenister and they blazed suddenly with hate.

'You'd found out, too, about me, hadn't you? You wondered where I went at night and you followed me . . . You told me so. You wanted to give back my diamonds to the people I'd taken them from. You promised if I did you would keep silent for Pam's sake. I promised, to keep you quiet because I was going to get you in the lethal chamber and stop you talking for ever. But this was a better plan. If you thought that I had been killed it wouldn't matter what you told the police, would it? They couldn't arrest a dead man!' He uttered another of his mirthless, horrible little chuckles.

Glenister opened his mouth to speak but Trevor Lowe stopped him with a gesture. Sir Reginald was talking as though he were alone, just putting his thoughts into words as he relived that night.

'I undressed Geoffrey, locked the study door; and took his clothes upstairs to my bedroom. His shirt was soaked in blood and I hid it in a cupboard. I had just done this when you came in to remind me of my promise.' He gave Glenister an evil look. 'If it had been possible I would have killed you, too. But it would have been too dangerous. I got rid of you and I changed quickly into Geoffrey's clothes. I took a clean dress shirt from my drawer and carried it, with my own discarded dinner suit, back to the study. But I forgot my studs and a collar and tie. It was too risky to go back. I hastily re-dressed

Geoffrey in the clean shirt and my clothes, put the body in the chair at my desk and went down to the garden.

'I strolled round to the terrace and found you and Pamela. I could have laughed aloud when I saw that neither of you suspected that I wasn't Geoffrey. After a little while I left you and went to Geoffrey's house and let myself in with his key. Wasn't that clever? I'd foiled all of you. I'd saved my beautiful diamonds . . .'

It was easy to see what had happened. Sir Reginald's always unbalanced brain had given away under the shock of discovery. He had gone right over the edge . . .

'Drincott nearly found me out,' the maniac went on. 'He was talking to me in the drawing room. He asked a question that Geoffrey could have answered easily but I couldn't. I saw by his expression that he'd guessed the truth. I shot him. Then I fired a bullet into the wall and threw my pistol through the window. I made up that story of the man in the raincoat who had fired through the window. It was such a good idea, wasn't it? I decided to keep it up by wearing this raincoat and tying a white scarf round my face. Rather like a thriller, eh? I like thrillers but the criminals aren't as clever as me . . .'

Suddenly his face changed. He passed a trembling hand across his eyes, and a troubled look came into them.

'What have I been talking about?' he asked mildly. 'I haven't been well, you know. The shock of poor Reginald's death upset me. I don't know what I'm saying sometimes. Did I tell you a lot of nonsense? Don't take any notice. I'm Geoffrey. Of course, I'm Geoffrey — Doctor Geoffrey Allerdyce.' He repeated this several times. 'Don't you believe anything else. It's all lies, lies! I'm not well — not well at all . . .'

'We understand,' said Lowe soothingly. 'Of course you are Doctor Allerdyce . . .'

And at that moment Shadgold came stumbling through the archway. He had his hand to his head and he was very unsteady.

'What happened?' he mumbled. 'My

head's as sore as hell! What's happened . . . ?'

'You were coshed,' began Lowe.

'Look out!' cried Glenister, but his warning came too late. The madman leapt out of his chair and dashed to the lamp. With a swift kick he smashed it against the wall. For a moment there was complete darkness and then the petrol container exploded with a report like a bomb. Blazing spirit was scattered in every direction.

Glenister tore off his coat and tried to beat out the flames and White went to his assistance. By the time they had succeeded and switched on a torch, Sir Reginald had vanished!

10

Sir Reginald Allerdyce hurried through the entrance to the Monk's Tomb, into the churchyard, closed the stone slab, and with a large stone that he found among the rank grass, hammered on the mechanism until he had jammed it. Now, when he twisted the projecting knob, nothing happened. He pushed against the opening with all his strength; but the slab was immovable.

He uttered a little breathless chuckle. That would bottle them up! They wouldn't be able to get out that way, not for a long time, anyhow — time enough for him to do what he had to do. And they couldn't get out through the lethal chamber. The iron door was too strong and solid to yield to anything short of a battering ram.

They were shut up in the tunnel!

He chuckled again, and set off for Abbey Lodge as quickly as he could. He had been a fool! It was queer how every now and again a mist seemed to envelope his brain and prevent him thinking clearly. And he'd talked too much! He'd given himself away. But now, for a spell, he was thinking clearly. Once they got out of the tunnel they'd be after him . . .

He stripped off the raincoat as he came to the kitchen garden. It was a pity that he had had to kill Greach. He would have been useful in this emergency. But the man could have been dangerous.

With a key he let himself in to the house by the back door. Rolling up the raincoat he thrust it into a cupboard in the scullery, went over to the sink and washed his hands and face, which were covered with grime from the passage.

When he had dried them on a towel, he walked quietly out into the hall, and tiptoed up the stairs. He didn't want to wake Leeker or any of the other servants.

At the door of Pamela's room he paused. Then he gently turned the handle and went in. The room was in darkness and he turned on the light switch. The light, softened by a pink silk shade, came on and revealed that his daughter was asleep.

He went softly over to the bed and looked down at her. His mind was as clear as crystal. The waves of acute madness had receded — for the moment.

She moved uneasily and her eyes, still heavy with sleep, opened . . . With a little cry of alarm, she started up as she saw him bending over her.

'Sh-s-s, Pam,' he whispered urgently. 'It's all right! It's only Uncle Geoffrey! Don't be frightened, and don't make a sound!'

'What is it? What's the matter?' she asked huskily, pushing back a wave of thick fair hair that had fallen over her forehead. 'Why are you here?'

'Do you feel strong enough to get up?' he asked.

She looked at him in surprise.

'Get up?' she repeated. 'Why?'

'I want you to get up and dress,' he answered. 'I want you to come with me. It's Norman . . . '

Her eyes widened in alarm.

'Norman? What's happened to Norman? Is he hurt . . . ?'

He nodded.

'The car skidded,' he answered gently. 'He'll be all right, but he's quite badly hurt and he's asking for you . . . '

'I'll come,' she broke in. 'I'll get dressed at once . . . ' She pushed back the bedcovers. 'Where is he?'

'I've taken him to a cottage,' he said. 'Not very far away. How long will you be?'

'Five minutes,' she answered.

'I'll wait for you down in the hall,' he said. 'Don't make a noise. There's no need to wake the household.' She nodded quickly.

'I'll hurry,' she said.

He went softly down the stairs. So far his plan was succeeding. With Pamela as an ally he could dictate terms to Glenister. Glenister was crazy about the girl. He had been willing to condone the robberies for her sake — to save her knowing that her father was a thief. But he had asked too high a price — the return of the stones. He would never give

206

them up. They were everything that he cared for in the world . . .

Pamela came quickly down to the hall.

'I'm ready,' she said. 'Are you sure he isn't seriously hurt?'

'No, no,' he reassured her. 'He'll recover, but it was a nasty smash . . . '

'Let's hurry,' she said. 'How do we get there?'

'I'll show you. Come this way . . . ' He led the way through to the kitchen. 'We'll have to go to my house first . . . '

'Why?' she demanded.

'To pick up my car,' he answered.

She was satisfied with the explanation. She was so worried about Norman that it never occurred to her to ask any questions. And the man she was with was her uncle . . .

Not for a single instant did she imagine that he was her father . . .

★ ★ ★

Trevor Lowe came back to the furnished vault followed by Arnold White. Shadgold, still holding his aching head, sat in the chair by the table, with Glenister perched on the table near him.

'Well?' asked Glenister.

Lowe shook his head.

'He's jammed the slab,' he announced. 'There's no way out through the Monk's Tomb. We tried everything but the slab won't budge an inch.'

'And there's no exit the other way,' said Glenister.

'The door of the lethal chamber is iron.'

'I know,' said the dramatist. 'I never put much faith on getting out that way . . . '

'So we're cooped up here like rats in a trap,' remarked Glenister.

'He can't get away,' put in the inspector. 'We're bound to get him . . . '

'In the meanwhile he's at large,' said Love, with a frown. 'A madman! There's no knowing what he'll do . . . '

'If we hammered on the iron door of the lethal chamber,' suggested White, 'surely somebody would hear us?'

'That's a chance but we'll have to wait until morning.' said his employer. 'The only person we might attract is Timms or the gardener . . . '

'Neither of them go near the kennels often,' put in Glenister. 'That was Greach's job . . . '

'And he's dead,' grunted Shadgold. 'Isn't there any chance of breaking a way out of that tomb?'

'Only if we had some kind of tools,' answered Lowe, 'It's quite impossible to do so without.'

There was a silence. The prospect was not very cheerful. Soon they wouldn't have any light. The vapour-lamp was smashed and the torch batteries were burning dim.

'I don't want to sound pessimistic,' said Shadgold, breaking the silence, 'but we could stay down here until we starve to death . . . '

'I don't think the position's as bad as that,' said Lowe. 'At least that lethal chamber is on the surface. If we take it in turns to bang on the iron door, sooner or later, somebody is bound to hear us.'

'I hope you're right,' said the inspector.

'There's not much use in starting too early,' continued Lowe. 'I should think about seven o'clock in the morning would be the best time . . . '

'It's not two yet,' broke in Glenister, looking at his watch. 'I suggest that we switch off the torch. We might need the light later. We might just as well wait in the dark.'

'You know,' said Arnold White, as Lowe put out the light, 'I can scarcely believe that that chap in the raincoat could be Sir Reginald. He was such a genial old fellow . . . '

'He appeared to be didn't he?' answered his employer. 'But there's not any doubt that he was mad. Outwardly, of course, until just now when his brain gave way completely, he seemed to be quite sane. There are numerous instances of mental cases of a similar nature. His kink was diamonds. You know, there are many collectors who are willing to go to any lengths, commit any crime, in order to secure a picture or other *objet d'art* for his collection. Not because he wants to show that he possesses such an object publicly, or exhibit it to his friends, but because he likes to gloat over it in secret.

That was Sir Reginald's desire. He had a passion for diamonds, not for their pecuniary value, but because he loved to possess them and handle them . . . '

'That's why we could never trace any of the stolen stuff,' said Shadgold. 'He never tried to dispose of any of it.'

'No, it's all in that safe there,' said Lowe. 'If we could trace every incident in his life we'd probably find a cause for the beginning of this insanity . . . '

'I think I can tell you that,' broke in Glenister.

'Some years ago he had a bad fall while he was hunting. He suffered a very severe injury to his head. He was unconscious for several days.'

'That would account for it,' agreed Trevor Lowe, 'The brain is a very delicate instrument, quite easily upset by many things. When did you first suspect that Sir Reginald was mixed up in these diamond robberies?'

'When I found out that he was in the habit of using my car at night,' said Glenister. 'That was about five days ago. I tackled him about the car, but to my

211

surprise he blandly denied that he'd used it. He suggested that it must've been Simms, the chauffeur, but I had actually seen him bring it back. I knew he was lying, but I'd no idea of the real truth. I kept a watch on him after that, and one night, when he went out, I followed him. He didn't take the car as I expected but he came here. I saw him enter the Monk's Tomb and I went in after him. He didn't see me, of course, I waited until he was well along the passage.

'I can't tell you my surprise when I saw this room and the table. It was covered with diamonds in every form and setting. He was running them through his fingers and crooning over them. It was really horrible! I could see then that he was crazy. And I could see something else. Those diamonds were stolen property. I had seen photographs of some of them in the papers.

'You can imagine what a terrible shock it was?'

'I certainly can,' said the dramatist. 'What did you do?'

'Nothing then,' answered Glenister. 'I

slipped away before he knew I was there. But I kept a pretty close watch on him after. I didn't know what to do. In the ordinary course I should have informed the police, but there was Pam. After all; he was her father . . . '

'You ought to have told the police,' said Shadgold.

In the darkness his voice held a note of disapproval. 'It might have prevented the murder of Doctor Allerdyce.'

'How was I to know that — then?' demanded Glenister. 'If you'd been in the same position, would you have acted differently, I wonder? I had to think of Pam. I didn't want any scandal for her sake . . . '

'You put yourself under suspicion,' interrupted the inspector.

'I know,' said Glenister. 'I guessed what you were all thinking. But that didn't worry me. I was only concerned to keep the truth from Pam . . . '

'She'll have to know now,' said Trevor Lowe. 'It will be impossible to keep it from her.'

'I suppose so.' Glenister sounded troubled.

'What did you do?' asked Lowe.

'I decided that I'd try and reason with him,' replied Glenister. 'I thought if I could get him to return the stolen diamonds the matter could be hushed up. I spoke to him about it on the afternoon before the murder. At first he went into a terrible rage and denied everything. He was like somebody possessed by the devil. But when I told him what I'd seen down here he quieted down. He asked me what I intended to do. I told him that if he would return all the diamonds to their rightful owners, I'd do nothing for Pam's sake.'

Glenister paused and cleared his throat.

'He promised me that he would,' he continued. 'But in the morning he was dead, or so I thought . . . '

'We all thought that,' grunted Shadgold.

'I thought that he'd been killed by somebody he'd hired to help him in the robberies — he told me he'd had to employ professional crooks to help him during our argument — and I must confess that I thought it was an easy way out. If I kept silent there was no reason why anyone should ever know the truth. I might be able to get hold of the diamonds when things had quieted down and send them back to their owners. And then came the murder of Superintendent Drincott . . . '

'You should have told us then,' said Trevor Lowe. 'After the murder of Drincott and the attempt on my life, you must have realised the seriousness of the situation.'

'I realised it well enough,' said Glenister, 'but Pamela had had a terrible shock over the supposed murder of her father. I was afraid that any further shock might do irreparable damage — perhaps kill her. I didn't know *what* to do . . . '

'What made you come down here tonight?' asked the inspector.

'I came to see if I could find any way of getting those diamonds,' said Glenister. 'It was lucky I did. When I got here, Sir Reginald was just going to shoot you, Mr. Lowe. He had that automatic at your head and I only just managed to grip his wrist and wrench the gun round before he could fire. He was so engrossed that he didn't hear me enter the vault. By jove, I'd never have believed that he was so strong . . . '

'And he's at large!' broke in Shadgold. 'He can get clean away while we're cooped up here . . . '

'But I don't think he will,' remarked Lowe. 'I don't think he'll try to get away.'

'What do you mean?' asked Shadgold. 'Surely while he's got the opportunity he'll . . . '

'Not without the diamonds,' said the dramatist. 'He won't go without them. They're the things that will hold him. He's mad about them, and that's more than a figure of speech. He will do anything, risk anything, to get them . . . '

'You mean that he'll come back here?' asked Glenister.

'I don't know what he'll do,' confessed Lowe. 'But I'm willing to bet every penny I possess that he won't go far without the diamonds.'

★　★　★

The car nosed its way slowly along a narrow lane. It was very narrow, with high rocky walls on each side. The surface was rutted and pitted and the car bumped and swayed as it moved slowly forward.

Pamela, worried and a little scared, turned to the man crouched over the wheel.

'Where *are* we?' she cried. 'I don't know this place at all. Surely we must be getting near the place where they took Norman?'

'We shan't be long now,' muttered Sir Reginald. 'This is a short cut . . . '

'But we've come such a long way already,' said Pamela. 'I don't understand . . . You're so — so strange, uncle . . . '

He only grunted in reply.

He had said very little since leaving Abbey Lodge. Pamela, full of questions about the accident, could get only brief unsatisfactory replies. They had collected the car from Doctor Allerdyce's house, and she still had no idea that the man with her was her father. The shock of being wakened in the middle of the night with the unexpected news of Glenister's injury, coming on the top of her recent illness, from which she hadn't entirely recovered, had left her weak and shaking.

If she had had the slightest inkling of the truth she might have collapsed entirely.

But that was to come later.

The lane ended in a wooden gate that blocked it completely, and the car came to a halt.

'Wait,' muttered Sir Reginald, and got out.

He opened the gate and dragged it back, revealing a weed-grown patch of ground that faced a small building that was neither a house nor a cottage but looked, in the light of the car's headlights, like a large shed. Sir Reginald came back and drove the car inside the gate.

'You can get out now, my dear,' he said, switching off the engine and the lights.

'But — but, uncle,' stammered Pamela in dismay, 'it isn't here, is it? Norman wasn't brought here . . . '

'You'll see, you'll see,' he answered evasively. 'Come along, take my arm.'

Unsteadily and wondering, she got out

of the car and with his assistance crossed over to the dark building. He took a key from his pocket and unlocked a narrow door at the side.

'Why are we going in here?' demanded Pamela, stopping. 'Norman *can't* be here. It's all dark . . . '

'Go in and I'll get a light,' said Sir Reginald. 'It's all right, my dear. You'll understand everything in a minute, I promise you. You've got to trust me.'

Reluctantly she crossed the threshold, and waited in the dark while he struck a match and lit an oil lamp that stood on a rough table in the middle of the bare, dusty floor.

'Now, Pam,' said Sir Reginald, 'I'm afraid that what I'm going to tell you will come as a big surprise. You must prepare yourself for a shock. I'm not your uncle Geoffrey. I'm your father!'

She stared at him. The light of the lamp swam in a dizzy whirl and she had to grasp the edge of the table to prevent herself from falling.

'It's all right, my dear,' he put his arm round her and supported her. 'I was afraid it would be a shock . . . '

She looked at him stupidly.

'I — I don't understand,' she whispered huskily, 'My father's dead — he was killed . . . '

'That was Geoffrey, dear,' he explained gently. 'It was Geoffrey who was killed. It was Norman who killed him.'

'Norman?' At first she didn't take it in. 'Norman? Oh, no . . . no. I'll never believe that, never. Norman wouldn't hurt anyone . . . '

'Norman Glenister killed Geoffrey,' repeated Sir Reginald. 'If I hadn't brought you away tonight he would have killed you.' She was recovering from the shock his words had given her. She still felt a little faint, and her legs seemed to have become too weak to support her, but her mind was clear.

'That's utter nonsense,' she replied. 'Why should Norman kill Uncle Geoffrey — why should he want to kill *me* — ? You must be mad!'

'Don't say that!' His voice was suddenly shrill. 'Don't ever say that, you don't understand! It's Glenister who's mad. He's been mad for a long time! Nobody knew it but me. That's why he tried to kill me and killed poor Geoffrey by mistake . . . '

Pamela gripped the edge of the table tighter. This was like a nightmare . . . She tried to force her brain to think, to take in what he was saying . . .

'All those diamonds Glenister gave you,' went on Sir Reginald, 'were stolen, do you understand? He is this man the police are searching for — the diamond thief. I found him out . . . '

'It isn't true,' she said. 'It *can't* be true . . . '

'I know how you feel, my dear,' he said gently. 'I would have saved you from this knowledge . . . I tried to — but he's dangerous, very dangerous! I had to get you away from Abbey Lodge or he would have killed you . . . '

She looked at him, her eyes clouded with doubt and perplexity. This thing, this terrible thing, he was telling her *couldn't* be true. There must be some horrible mistake. Norman would never harm her — would never *wish* to harm her. He had always been so gentle and considerate . . . Other people had thought him hard and arrogant, but she had seen beneath the surface . . . It was impossible that he could be a thief — impossible that he could have killed anyone . . .

Sir Reginald was watching her keenly.

'It's very hard to believe, my dear,' he said, 'but why should I tell you if it were not true?'

He sounded so convincing that she wavered. If Norman were really mad . . .? But it was ridiculous. Norman was always so calm and sane . . . She remembered how he had talked to her and tried to soothe her after the shock of her father's death. He couldn't have behaved as he had done if he had been responsible . . .

'You must be wrong,' she whispered, 'you must be. You may think that you aren't, but you are . . . '

'I wish you were right,' he said.

'Where is Norman?' she asked.

He shook his head.

'I don't know,' he answered. 'But don't worry. He will never find you here.'

'But we can't stop here,' she exclaimed.

'What is this place?'

'It belongs to me,' he said. 'Nobody will think of looking for you here. You are quite safe . . . '

'What do you mean?' she asked in dismay. 'How long are we going to stop here?'

'Until Glenister is no longer able to harm you,' he replied. 'It will not be long. I have brought food and drink in the car . . . '

She looked round the bare dusty shed. There was not even a chair . . .

'I'll not stay,' she said firmly.

His face changed. His eyes hardened and his mouth set.

'I know what is best for you,' he retorted. 'You'll do as I tell you!'

'I'm not going to stay here,' she declared. She tried to walk to the door but her legs gave way and she had to clutch at him to prevent herself from falling. The whole place seemed to shift and quiver as she fell limply into his supporting arms . . .

11

'Try again,' said Trevor Lowe.

He, White, Detective-Inspector Shadgold, and Glenister were grouped round the iron door inside the lethal chamber. For the past hour they had taken it in turns to hammer on the iron plates in the hope that someone would hear. But without result.

Glenister clenched his fists and beat a thunderous tattoo on the door. It sounded loud to them in the confined space of the lethal chamber but it was probably very much less loud outside.

He kept it up until his hands were sore and then Arnold White took over.

'Even if someone does hear,' said Lowe, 'it's not going to be easy for them to get us out. Sir Reginald has the key. They'll have to force the door.'

'It'll be something if only someone *hears* us,' grunted Shadgold. 'Let me have a go!'

He hammered and kicked at the iron door but there was no response from outside.

'We dare not stop,' said Lowe as he took the inspector's place, 'because that might be the moment when somebody was within earshot.'

It was Glenister who suddenly gave a shout.

'Stop!' he cried. 'Somebody called. I heard them!'

Lowe stopped beating on the door.

A faint voice came to their straining ears.

'What's up in there?' it asked. 'Is that you, Greach?'

'We're locked in,' shouted Glenister. 'Who is that?'

'This is Timms,' answered the voice outside. 'Is that Captain Glenister?'

'Yes,' replied Glenister. 'Can you get the door open?'

'Greach may 'ave the key, sir,' shouted the chauffeur. 'I'll go and see if I can . . . '

'You won't find Greach,' said Glenister. 'You'll have to break the lock somehow.'

There was a short silence.

'It ain't goin' ter be easy, sir,' called Timms. 'I might be able ter drill a 'ole an' cut round the lock with an 'acksaw . . . '

'We don't care what you do so long as you get us out!' shouted Shadgold.

'Lumme!' cried the chauffeur. ''Ow many are yer?'

'There are four of us,' called Glenister. 'Hurry up and see what you can do.'

'Right you are, sir,' shouted Timms. 'I'll go an' get me tools.'

It seemed an age before they heard him again.

''Ere goes, sir,' he called. 'I'll start drillin'.'

'Lucky,' remarked the dramatist, 'that the door's iron and not steel. It shouldn't take him very long.'

But it took Timms the better part of three quarters of an hour before he succeeded in cutting round the lock that held the close-fitting door shut. He stared in astonishment as he finally pulled open the door and they came blinking out into the sunshine.

''Ow did yer manage ter get in there, sir?' he asked. 'What's 'appened ter

Greach? 'E's usually about . . . '

'Greach is dead,' said Glenister. 'His body is in there . . . '

'It mustn't be touched until the police have been,' interrupted Shadgold. 'I'll phone to Bracken as soon as we get to the house. You haven't seen Sir — er — Doctor Allerdyce this morning, have you?'

Timms shook his head.

'I ain't seen no one,' he answered. 'I was just going along ter the garidge when I 'eard you bangin' on that there door. Couldn't make it out at first . . . '

'It would be a good thing if you kept this to yourself,' said the inspector.

They left the obviously bewildered chauffeur to collect his tools and carry them back to the garage; and made their way across the kitchen garden to the house. In the kitchen they found Leeker talking to an agitated housemaid.

The butler turned quickly as they came in and his face expressed his surprise.

'Goodness me, you startled me!' exclaimed the old man. 'I didn't know you was out, Captain Glenister . . . '

'We'd like some tea and some breakfast as soon as you can get it, Leeker,' said Glenister. 'I'm going to get a wash . . . '

'Good idea,' said Lowe. 'We must look like scarecrows . . . '

'I'll join you after I've phoned,' said Shadgold. 'Bracken must be notified at once. We must put out an all stations call for — well, you know who I mean?'

'Excuse me, sir,' put in Leeker, 'but have you seen anything of Miss Pamela?'

'Isn't she in her room?' demanded Glenister.

'No, sir.' It was the housemaid who answered. 'I took up her morning tea but she wasn't there. I was just tellin' Mr. Leeker . . . '

Glenister turned a troubled face to Lowe.

'Can anything have happened to her?' he said. 'She wouldn't have got up unless . . . '

Lowe's face was just as troubled as he replied seriously:

'I don't like it — I don't like it at all. Come up to the drawing room. We can't discuss it here.'

Glenister nodded, and they followed him up the stairs to the hall. When they reached the drawing room, Trevor Lowe went on:

'He might have taken the girl to use as a bargaining proposition . . .'

'How do you mean?'

'In order to get those diamonds . . .'

'But — Pam's his own daughter, man! Surely he wouldn't . . . ?'

'He's not normal — don't forget that. We're not dealing with a sane man . . .'

Glenister's face went white.

'You — you don't mean — that Pam could be in any danger . . . ?'

Lowe's face was grave.

'Sir Reginald is a man with one idea,' he answered. 'Those diamonds. They mean more to him than anything else in the world. If it came to a choice . . .' He stopped.

'Good God, this is terrible!' Glenister struck his hand on the back of a chair. 'What can we do? We must find them at once . . .'

'Steady,' broke in the dramatist. 'We don't know yet that she's with him . . .'

'Then where is she?' demanded Glenister. 'She wouldn't have gone out on her own . . . she wasn't well enough. We've got to do something . . . '

'Do you know anywhere he could have taken her?'

'Geoffrey Allerdyce's cottage?'

Lowe shook his head.

'I doubt if he'd go there,' he answered. 'He'd realise that would be the first place we'd think of . . . '

'But he doesn't know that we managed to get out of the underground tunnel,' said Glenister.

'No, but he'll take the possibility into account,' replied the dramatist. 'Although he's insane, we've got to remember that he's by no means a fool. The two things don't go together, you know. He has all the cunning of a madman, plus a very efficient organising ability. We've evidence of that in the way that he planned and carried out these diamond robberies . . . ' Shadgold came in quickly.

'I've been on to Bracken,' he said. 'The net will be spread wide. The pompous fool!' he added angrily. 'He blames me for the whole thing . . . '

'Never mind about that,' broke in Glenister. 'It's Pam we've got to worry about . . . '

'We've no idea that she's in any danger,' began the inspector, but Glenister interrupted him.

'We've got to find her,' he said. 'If this maniac . . . ' he stopped as Leeker came in.

'We've just found this in the broom cupboard in the scullery, sir,' he said, and held out a crumpled raincoat. 'I thought that . . . '

'That's the raincoat he was wearing!' cried Glenister.

'That settles it,' said Lowe. 'He *has* been here . . . Thank you, Leeker.'

Shadgold took the raincoat from the old man, and the butler withdrew. He made a rapid search of the pockets but they were empty. He put the coat down on a chair.

'I'm going along to Doctor Allerdyce's house,' he said. 'There may be something there that will help us . . . '

'We'll all go,' said Glenister, but Lowe shook his head.

'Let Arnold go with you,' he said. 'I think we should stop here . . . '

'Why?' demanded Glenister. 'You don't expect him to come back here, surely?'

'We've got to be prepared for anything,' answered the dramatist. 'His main object is to get hold of those diamonds. He can't get into the vault from the Monk's Tomb because he's jammed the entrance. And he won't risk the lethal chamber entrance while he thinks we are still down there . . . '

'What do you think he's going to do, then?'

Lowe shook his head.

'I don't know,' he declared candidly. 'But I don't think it would be wise to leave this house unguarded.'

Glenister shrugged his shoulders.

'Perhaps, you're right,' he admitted. He raised a shaking hand to his chin and rubbed it nervously. 'I must have a drink,' he said. 'I need something to pull myself together. There's some brandy in the dining room. I'll get it. We could all do with something!'

He went out quickly.

'Looks almost at the end of his tether,' said the inspector. 'I must say that I could do with a drop of something, myself.'

'We're all suffering from strained nerves,' said Lowe, 'but, of course, Glenister's had a worse time than we have . . . '

'Do you think the girl's in any danger?' asked Shadgold.

'A man in Sir Reginald's state is unpredictable,' answered the dramatist, 'he's capable of anything . . . '

Glenister came back with a tray containing glasses and a bottle of Hennessy. Putting the tray down, he poured out four large brandies and passed them round.

'This'll do us good,' he said. 'They've laid the table for breakfast, but I don't think I could eat anything now.'

He swallowed a gulp of brandy.

'I could,' remarked the inspector, 'but I haven't time.' He drank his brandy and smacked his lips. 'That was good,' he said. 'Come along, White, we'll get along to Allerdyce's house.'

Arnold put down his empty glass on the tray and followed him out the door.

'Let us know if you find anything,' called Lowe. 'I don't expect that they will,' he added, turning to Glenister.

'I wish we could do something instead of just sitting here,' said Glenister. 'It seems such a waste of time . . . '

'It's no good rushing about for the sake of it,' said Lowe with reason. 'We've no idea where to look for Sir Reginald. We've got to wait for him to make the first move — and be ready when he does.'

There was sense in what he said, and Glenister, in spite of his anxiety, had to admit it. But the time dragged slowly by and nothing happened. Leeker came to inform them that breakfast had been served in the dining room, and although they were glad of the hot tea, they left the food untasted.

Shadgold and White came back with the information that Doctor Allerdyce's car had gone from his garage, and there were signs that somebody had been in the house recently. But there was nothing to show where the car had gone.

'I'll bet that he's going to try and make a getaway,' grunted the inspector. 'If he comes back to try and get those diamonds, I'll eat my hat!'

'Don't make rash promises!' retorted Lowe.

★   ★   ★

Detective-Inspector Shadgold might have altered his mind if he could have seen Sir Reginald Allerdyce at that particular moment.

Concealed by the leafy branches of a majestic oak tree, he watched through a pair of field glasses the courtyard and the door to the lethal chamber. He hadn't actually seen Timms rescue Glenister, Lowe, Shadgold and White — he hadn't reached his point of vantage in time for that — but he could see that the iron door was open and the patch where the lock had been cut out.

But he was in time to witness the police, in the persons of Detective-Inspector Bracken; Sergeant Swires and two constables, bring out the bodies of 'Black' Berman and Greach. He saw the police-doctor and the photographer come out of the lethal chamber, and watched the ambulance drive away with all that remained of the men he had killed.

But they couldn't get at the diamonds. They were still locked up in the safe. He had slammed the door shut before Glenister had arrived to spoil his plans . . .

Glenister!

He was responsible for all this. If it hadn't been for him, he would never have been suspected. There had been Geoffrey, of course, but he had dealt with Geoffrey, and without Glenister's interference he would have got away with it — at least long enough to get away with his beloved diamonds.

And he'd do that yet!

There was nobody in the vault at the moment, but he couldn't make a move yet. Would they put a guard in it? It was more than likely. But he held a trump card in Pamela.

He had locked her in the shed and the

door was strong and the lock a stout one. She would be quite safe there. He had brought blankets in the car and he had tucked her up warmly on the floor. It had alarmed him a little when she had fainted in his arms; but she had recovered although she was still weak and frightened.

He had no wish to harm her, but the diamonds came before everything. He had tried to explain to her — laying all the blame on Glenister — but he could see that she didn't believe him. She didn't realise the truth but she was frightened of him. He could see it in her eyes . . .

And it was all Glenister's fault!

He'd make Glenister pay!

So long as he'd got Pam, he could force Glenister to do anything he asked. That was the cleverness of the idea! Glenister would do anything for Pam . . .

It was lucky he had thought of the shed. He had bought it a long time ago and no one knew that it belonged to him. He had used it to meet the crooks he had hired to help him in the robberies. They had never known who he really was

— except Berman.

Berman hadn't been satisfied, like the others, with what he had paid him. He had wanted more. He had found out that he was Sir Reginald Allerdyce, and discovered the secret of the Monk's Tomb . . .

Well, Berman was dead!

He would have to be very careful. The police would be looking for him, but he had eluded them so far and he could do it again. They would never expect him to come back for the diamonds . . . The fools! Did they imagine that he would leave that safe full of glittering beauty to fall into the hands of those who hadn't the brains to appreciate their eternal loveliness?

Carefully he climbed down from the huge oak tree. He had no fear of being seen. The tree stood on the edge of a small copse and it was unlikely that anybody would be looking for him here. It would be the roads and lanes that they would expect to find him, if they imagined that he was still in the district.

They had probably discovered by now

that the car had gone from Geoffrey's garage. They would think that he was a long way from Abbey Lodge. And they would never find the shed where he had taken Pam. The lane leading to that led nowhere else and was never used.

What he wanted now was a telephone. There was one in Greach's room by the kennels. Could he get at it or would the police be guarding it? If he approached the kennels from the back, it might be possible. The ground was rough and overgrown with brambles and blackberries, which would offer him ample cover. Provided there was nobody actually on guard in the building, he could make it . . .

He moved cautiously forward. He hadn't far to go. The bushes extended almost to the copse where the oak tree grew. The brambles tore at his clothing and scratched his hands and face but he scarcely noticed, and at last he reached the back of the kennels.

Here he paused and took stock. There was nobody about, He couldn't see the courtyard because of the buildings but he had no intention of going into the courtyard.

Greach had occupied a room over the dispensary, a low-built building but higher than the kennels. He could hear the hounds whimpering and he wondered if anyone had thought to feed them. Curiously enough the thought worried him. Those hounds had been his pride. What would happen to them? Glenister would look after them, but Glenister wouldn't be in a position to. He had forgotten that for the moment. No doubt the Hunt would see that they were properly looked after . . .

He was facing the back of the dispensary now. Even if anyone had been looking out of the windows they couldn't have seen him. The thick, high bushes formed too good a screen.

And the building almost butted on to them. There was a door to the dispensary and the key was in his pocket. Only he and Greach had possessed a key and he had taken Greach's key after he had killed him, as he had taken the key to the lethal chamber.

Now was the risky part. He left the cover of the bushes and with both eyes and ears on the alert, he drew the key of the dispensary door from his pocket and inserted it in the lock.

With a twist of his wrist he unlocked the door. A turn of the handle and a gentle push and it opened. He slipped inside, closed the door, and stood listening.

All was silent inside.

He crossed the dispensary with its shelves of bottles and jars. It was from here that he had taken the flask of hydrocyanic acid. It was a pity that had gone wrong . . .

At one side of the room a narrow wooden stair led upwards to the room Greach had occupied. He paused at the foot and listened again.

Nothing stirred above.

He tiptoed up the stairs. There was no door at the top. They led straight into the room. A single glance showed him that it was tenantless.

But the police had been here. Drawers had been opened and the contents tipped out. Even the narrow bed against one wall had been stripped. The room had been subjected to a thorough search.

Sir Reginald Allerdyce uttered a soft chuckle. Well, they hadn't found anything because there was nothing here to find.

He went over to the window and looked out on to the courtyard through the thin net curtains.

A bored-looking constable was sitting on an upturned box near the door of the lethal chamber. He was smoking a cigarette and yawning.

So they *had* put a guard in the courtyard!

But they had chosen the wrong place! No doubt the idea was to prevent anyone getting through the lethal chamber and down to the vault.

He chuckled softly again. He wasn't ready for that yet! When he was, did they think that a young policeman was going to stop him?

On a shelf near the head of the bed stood the telephone. It was connected with the exchange and he picked up the receiver and gave the number of Abbey Lodge.

12

Glenister prowled restlessly up and down the drawing room, smoking one cigarette after another in an endless chain. He looked tired and drawn, keeping going entirely on his reserve of nervous energy.

Trevor Lowe sat in an easy chair and if he looked outwardly calm, within he was a greatly disturbed and troubled man.

But there was nothing to be done at the moment.

Shadgold had gone to help Bracken with his efforts to find Sir Reginald. Arnold White was leaning on the stone balustrade of the terrace, staring gloomily on to the sundrenched lawn.

The day was as hot as the previous one. From a cloudless sky the sun blazed down on the baked earth. Even the long, cool-looking drawing room was hot enough to bring little beads of perspiration out on their foreheads.

Shadgold and White had had something to eat, but neither Lowe nor Glenister had eaten anything. But they had got through two large pots of coffee.

There had been no message from the patrols who were out looking for Sir Reginald. Roadblocks had been set up on all the ways out of Long Norton but without result.

Trevor Lowe had not expected that there would be. If Sir Reginald had intended to make his getaway he would have been well away before the patrols had been notified and the roadblocks set up. And he wouldn't have taken Pamela with him. He had planned something entirely different, something that involved the girl; and all they could do was to wait until they knew what the madman had in his warped mind.

It was at the dramatist's suggestion that a watch had been set on the lethal chamber. If Sir Reginald was planning to get the diamonds — and Lowe was convinced that that was his object — the only way down to the vault now that the Monk's Tomb was useless was through the iron door. After much argument, he had also persuaded them to set a watch in the churchyard, just in case any attempt should be made smash a way into the tomb. Lowe was very doubtful if there would be, something subtler would be tried, but every precaution should be taken.

'I can't stand much more of this,' muttered Glenister, suddenly stopping abruptly in his ceaseless patrol of the room. 'Isn't there *anything* we can do?'

'I wish I could think of something,' answered the dramatist, 'but I can't. I'm sure that we shall hear something soon, but until we do . . . '

'While we sit here waiting, what's happening to Pamela?' demanded Glenister. 'She was ill before she left here — God knows what she is now . . . '

'I can understand how you feel,' began Lowe sympathetically, when the sound of the telephone ringing interrupted him.

Glenister was at the door in two strides and wrenched it open. Leeker was just picking up the receiver.

'Yes, sir,' he said as the receiver

chattered. 'Who shall I say wishes to speak to him?'

'What is it, Leeker?' demanded Glenister.

'Someone for you, sir,' began the old man. 'I don't know . . . '

Glenister took the receiver from his hand before he could get any further.

'Glenister here,' he said curtly. 'Who's that?'

The telephone chattered again. Leeker had gone away, but Lowe had come to the door of the drawing room. He saw Glenister's face change and the sudden tightening of his hand on the receiver.

'What have . . . ?' he began and stopped as the telephone continued to chatter. 'Very well,' said Glenister in a toneless voice after several minutes when the chattering ceased. 'Yes . . . Yes . . . All right, I will . . . '

He hung up the receiver and turned away from the telephone. His face was like thunder. His eyes held an angry glint and his hands were clenched. And then he saw Lowe and by a supreme effort he

246

managed to wipe all expression from his face.

'Was it anything important?' asked the dramatist.

Glenister shook his head.

'No,' he answered but he avoided Lowe's eyes. 'Only a — a friend of mine . . . Wants me to look in one evening soon . . . I said I would,' he passed the tip of his tongue over his lips. 'I think I'll go up and lie down for a bit,' he continued. 'I feel . . . rather tired . . . '

He turned abruptly away and went up the stairs two at a time. Lowe heard the slam of a door from above,

Glenister was not a good liar. As plainly as if he'd said so, the dramatist knew that that telephone message had come from Sir Reginald Allerdyce. He had demanded something from Glenister — and Glenister had agreed, obviously because Pamela had been used as the inducement.

This was what Lowe had been expecting. That it was connected with the diamonds, he was certain, but he was also certain that all the tortures ever devised wouldn't make Glenister divulge what it was while the girl's safety depended on his doing whatever it was he had been asked.

And Lowe couldn't find it in his heart to blame him. But he was determined that whatever Sir Reginald's plan was he was not going to get away with it.

★ ★ ★

The constable on duty in the courtyard outside the lethal chamber was fed up. Because every available man had been taken to help in the search for Sir Reginald Allerdyce he far exceeded his normal eight hours of duty. It was true that sandwiches and coffee had been sent to him, but he was tired. The heat had not helped, although he had kept in the shade as much as possible, the air itself was stifling. Now that it was almost dark the atmosphere was a little colder.

Nothing had happened to break the monotony of his vigil. Nobody had come near the courtyard except Timms, the chauffeur, who had plied him with curious questions that he was unable to answer. They hadn't told him anything — only that he was to keep an eye on the door to the lethal chamber and allow nobody in. If anyone tried to reach it, he was to blow his whistle.

One thing was certain, they couldn't expect him to carry on all night. They'd have to find someone to relieve him.

He turned his head as he heard the sound of an approaching footstep. This was probably his relief . . .

He went over to meet the man who had just entered the courtyard . . .

★   ★   ★

Sir Reginald Allerdyce put down the large suitcase he was carrying on the floor of the vault. He gave a little chuckle as he looked up at the stern face of Glenister in the light of the electric hand lamp that he had put on the table.

'How did you get rid of that policeman?' he asked.

'That's my business;' replied Glenister curtly. 'I want to get away from here. I've carried out my part of the bargain — now tell me where Pamela is!'

Sir Reginald chuckled again.

'Not yet,' he said, 'not until I've got the diamonds.'

'Hurry up. then,' snapped Glenister.

Sir Reginald picked up the lamp and carried it over to the safe. He spun the dial with the ease of long practice and pulled the heavy door open. As he flashed the light of the lamp into the interior, Glenister saw that it was empty except for a series of narrow shelves at the back. These were covered with velvet and on them were heaped the result of the numerous robberies. They glittered and shot sparks of rainbow-hued fire.

'There they are, my beautiful stones,' whispered Sir Reginald. 'My lovely diamonds . . . '

Glenister brought over the suitcase.

'Get them packed up and let's go,' he said.

Sir Reginald turned. His eyes were glittering with a light that was almost like the gems on the shelves. In one hand he held an automatic.

'You're not going,' he snarled. 'I never meant that you should leave here. But for you I shouldn't be in this position . . . '

'Don't be a fool,' said Glenister.

'A fool?' Sir Reginald chuckled. 'You're the fool to expect that I ever intended to let you live . . . '

'Pamela . . . ' began Glenister, and the other laughed. It was a high-pitched, shrill laugh.

'You'll never see Pamela again,' he retorted. 'I shall tell Leeker where to find her, after I've left here. But you will be dead!' His voice rose to a scream. 'Dead!' he repeated, *'Dead!'*

'Drop that gun!'

Sir Reginald, his lips curled back from his teeth in an animal snarl, turned his head in the direction from whence the curt order had come. Shadgold had come through the arch at the other end of the vault and was covering him with an automatic. Behind him loomed the figures of Trevor Lowe and Arnold White.

'Drop that gun!' ordered Shadgold again.

And like lightning, Glenister acted. His

arm shot out and he gripped the gun in Sir Reginald's hand and wrenched it from him. Sir Reginald pulled the trigger at the same moment and the sound of the report echoed through the chamber.

'If you don't let me go,' screamed the madman, his face distorted, 'you'll never see Pamela again. She'll starve to death! D'you hear? She'll starve . . . '

'She'll do nothing of the kind,' broke in Trevor Lowe. 'By now she should be back at Abbey Lodge . . . '

'So you tricked me!' Sir Reginald turned a face that was no longer human towards Glenister. 'You want to rob me of my diamonds! But you shan't! You shan't! You'll never part me from them!'

Glenister tried to stop him but he was too late! Sir Reginald swung round, leapt into the safe and pulled the door shut!

Glenister seized the handle and tried to turn it, but it was immovable.

Sir Reginald Allerdyce had spoken the truth. He couldn't be parted from his diamonds now. He would die in the steel coffin in which he had shut himself with the gems that had been his life's desire.

It was three hours later. Glenister, Lowe, Arnold White, and Shadgold sat in the drawing room at Abbey Lodge. Pamela, worn out from her ordeal, was in bed and asleep. They all felt worn out, and were grateful for the stiff portions of John Haig that Glenister had given them.

There was nothing they could do to save the madman who had chosen death rather than be parted from the diamonds he had risked so much to acquire. Only an expert could open the safe without knowing the combination. Shadgold had sent for one but by the time he arrived, it would be too late. The air in that confined space would not last long . . .

It was Shadgold who had found Pamela. He had got in touch with the Yard, giving them a list of the crooks whom Sir Reginald had employed, taken from the red book Lowe had found in the drawer of the table in the vault. One of these had told the officer of the shed where he had met Sir Reginald. When this had been relayed to Shadgold, he had gone to the shed and found the frightened girl.

As soon as Glenister realised that she was safe, he had informed them of Sir Reginald's telephone message. He had threatened that unless Glenister helped him to get the diamonds, Pamela would suffer. Glenister had agreed to get rid of the constable on duty and meet Sir Reginald in the vault. Glenister had promised for Pamela's sake, but the promise had been made under duress and when Shadgold had told him that Pamela was safe he had told them everything.

Shadgold had got rid of the constable by the simple method of relieving him of his duty. They had taken up their position in the other passage leading to the vault before Glenister had notified Sir Reginald that the coast was clear.

'And that's the end of it,' said Trevor Lowe. 'I should marry Miss Allerdyce as soon as possible, Glenister, and take her away somewhere for a while. She'll soon recover from the shock in different surroundings.'

'I will — don't worry about that,' said Glenister.

'I wonder why he made those two attempts on your life, Mr. Lowe?' said Shadgold; helping himself to another Haig.

'I asked him some rather pointed questions about that changed shirt,' replied the dramatist. 'He thought I'd found out that it was Geoffrey Allerdyce who was killed . . . '

'You guessed, didn't you?' said Glenister.

'Yes, but not at once. I was puzzled why there wasn't any blood on the shirt. The only solution to that was that it had been changed after the stabbing. But the dead man couldn't have done that himself. There was only one sensible answer . . . '

'Well, I'll bet that Bracken will have an apoplectic stroke when he hears all about it,' remarked Shadgold with great satisfaction. 'I don't think I've ever disliked anyone so much!'

He took a deep drink of Haig and settled back in his chair with a sigh of content.

THE END

We do hope that you have enjoyed reading this large print book.

Did you know that all of our titles are available for purchase?

We publish a wide range of high quality large print books including:
Romances, Mysteries, Classics
General Fiction
Non Fiction and Westerns

Special interest titles available in large print are:
The Little Oxford Dictionary
Music Book, Song Book
Hymn Book, Service Book

Also available from us courtesy of Oxford University Press:
Young Readers' Dictionary
(large print edition)
Young Readers' Thesaurus
(large print edition)

For further information or a free brochure, please contact us at:
Ulverscroft Large Print Books Ltd.,
The Green, Bradgate Road, Anstey,
Leicester, LE7 7FU, England.
Tel: (00 44) **0116 236 4325**
Fax: (00 44) **0116 234 0205**

THE COPPER BULLET

John Russell Fearn

Dr. Bland retires to his office to rest, complaining of a headache. But later, his fellow scientists find him slumped over his desk — dead. In his forehead is a round hole, edged with burn marks. He has apparently shot himself — but there is no sign of a gun. The only clue is a copper bullet, of the type used in a .38 revolver. There is no cartridge cover — indicating that the bullet *has* been fired, and then put there . . .

THE UNIVERSAL HOLMES

Richard A. Lupoff

Sherlock Holmes is probably the most popular figure in world literature. For more than a century his adventures have been chronicled in books, on the stage and radio, in motion pictures and television. These Sherlock Holmes adventures show Conan Doyle's detective not only in his earliest days, but also in connection with the works of other authors — Edgar Allan Poe, Edgar Rice Burroughs, H. P. Lovecraft — as Holmes proves himself to be truly *The Universal Holmes*.